BANG GOES A TROLL

BY THE BEASTLY BOYS
ILLUSTRATED BY JONNY DUDDLE

SIMON AND SCHUSTER

First published in Great Britain in 2009
by Simon and Schuster UK Ltd
A CBS COMPANY
This paperback edition published in 2011.

Simon & Schuster UK Ltd
1st Floor, 222 Gray's Inn Road, London WC1X 8HB.

ISBN: 978-0-85707-181-1

1 3 5 7 9 10 8 6 4 2

Printed in the UK by CPI Cox & Wyman, Reading, Berkshire RG1 8EX

www.simonandschuster.co.uk

TONIGHT,

LOOK UP AT THE MOON.

LOOK AT IT CLOSELY.

STARE AT IT.

NOW ASK YOURSELF:

AM I FEELING BRAVE?

BEASTLY
BUSINESS

CHAPTER ONE

High on a snowy mountaintop, a blizzard was
howling. A tall man in a long fur coat staggered
knee-deep through the snow, glancing into the
mouths of caves. He gripped his high fur collar,
shielding his face from the wind, and peered
down into a hole in the ground. 'This is the
one,' he muttered. 'Blud! Bone! Over here!'

'Coming, Baron Marackai.'

Two men were trudging towards him through
the snow. One was small and was clutching a
rifle. The other was big with a frosted beard
and was dragging a long black hose.

'Stick the hose down here, Bone,' Baron
Marackai ordered.

The big man Bone poked the end of the hose into the hole in the ground. He twisted a nozzle and thick black oil started pouring out into the mountain.

The three men waited silently as oil glugged from the hose. Snowflakes were swirling around them, whitening their hair and clothes.

'It's fr-fr-freezing up here,' the small man muttered. The rifle in his hands was rattling and a snotty icicle hung from his nose. He glanced down the mountainside, his eyes following the hose to an oil tanker and a cattle truck parked on an icy track. 'Can I w-w-wait in the tr-truck, Sir?'

'Stay where you are, Blud, you snivelling runt,' Baron Marackai ordered.

'Yes, B-Baron M-Marackai. Sorry B-Baron M-Marackai,' the small man muttered.

The Baron turned to Bone and stamped his serpent-skin boot. 'Hurry up!' he yelled.

Bone looked down into the hole. 'Nearly finished, Sir.' The hose gurgled and he shook black oily drips from its end.

'Is that the whole tanker full?'

'It's all in there, Sir.'

'Splendid,' the Baron said. 'Blud, pass me the matches. It's time to smoke out the trolls.'

Blud fumbled in his jacket pocket and handed Baron Marackai a crumpled box of matches.

Baron Marackai struck a match and its flame fizzed, then went out. He tried to strike another but it snapped in two. 'These are old matches, Blud!'

'I found them on the reception desk at the hotel,' Blud told him.

'You useless fool,' Baron Marackai muttered. He took the remaining matches from the box and struck them all at once. They sputtered into flame and he dropped them down the hole. There was a whooshing sound as the oil caught fire and flames roared underground. All across the snowy mountain, thick black smoke began billowing from holes and caves.

'Get ready!' Baron Marackai ordered. He hid behind Bone, using the big man as a human shield. Blud crouched beside him.

'Not you, Blud,' Baron Marackai said. 'You're the shooter!' He pushed the small man into the open.

Blud stood shivering in the wind and snow, his eyes darting from left to right as he pointed his rifle from one smoking cave to another.

From inside the mountain came the sounds of underground beasts: growls and squeals, bellows and squawks. Beasts came hurrying from caves, trying to escape the smoke. An ice-bear bounded out into the snow, roaring. A vampire owl flew screeching into the air. A giant wraith spider scurried out, hissing.

'It's the trolls I want!' the Baron shouted.

'There's one!' Bone called.

From a smoking cave, a huge green troll charged out on all fours, swiping the air with its long tusks. It roared, snorting smoke from its nostrils. The troll saw Blud and stood tall, beating its chest. 'Oof! Oof! Oof!'

'Help!' Blud cried.

Baron Marackai peered out from behind Bone, pointing. 'Shoot it, you moron!'

Blud aimed his rifle at the troll. His teeth rattled as he squeezed the trigger and fired. A feathered tranquillizer dart shot out and struck the troll on the chest.

The troll stumbled, then toppled to the ground with a thud. It lay in the snow, face down, unconscious.

Blud spun round as another big green troll ran from the mouth of a cave.

'Aim between its eyes!' the Baron shouted.

Blud fired another tranquillizer dart, hitting the troll on the arm. It tumbled into the snow. Another troll burst out and Blud fired again. The feathered dart hit the troll on the nose.

'Behind you!' Bone called.

Two more trolls charged out from the smoke-filled mountain and Blud fired twice. The trolls fell, one on top of the other.

Troll after troll burst from the caves. There was oofing and roaring, and the whizz and crack of tranquillizer darts firing from the rifle. One by one they toppled into the snow.

Slowly, the mountain fell silent and the

smoke began to clear. More than twenty trolls lay tranquillized and unconscious on the ground.

'Splendid!' Baron Marackai said, stepping out from behind Bone.

He walked through the snow to one of the trolls and kicked it with his serpent-skin boot. 'Sleeping like a baby,' he said. 'Bone, pick out five young ones and load them on to the cattle truck.'

Bone trudged over to inspect the tranquillized trolls. 'How do I tell which are the young ones, Sir? They all look big and ugly.'

'The young ones have the softest skin,' Baron Marackai told him.

Bone knelt down and pinched a troll's cheek, tugging its thick rubbery skin.

Blud skittered over to the Baron. 'What are we going to do with them, Sir?' he asked.

The Baron rubbed his hands together. 'We shall use them in the Predatron,' he said.

'The Predatron!' Blud said excitedly.

'These stupid beasts won't stand a chance.'

'But what if we get caught, Sir?' Blud asked. The small man glanced shiftily from side to side. 'What if you-know-who find out?'

'I have prepared for that,' Baron Marackai said, grinning.

The Baron stroked the small stump of flesh on his right hand where his little finger was missing. He held his hand up. 'Now, repeat after me. Death to the RSPCB!'

Blud and Bone turned down their little fingers then held up their right hands. 'Death to the RSCPC!' they said.

'The RS*PCB*, you numbskulls!'

The Baron picked up two handfuls of snow and pushed them in the men's faces. 'Now load those trolls on the truck! I have important business to attend to.'

Blud and Bone wiped the snow from their eyes and watched curiously as the Baron strode off across the mountain. He was peering into the caves.

'Where are you?' the Baron called. 'Come to Marackai.'

He glanced over at a small hole about twenty metres away. The head of a creature with pointy ears and large white eyes was poking from it.

The Baron waved. 'Coo-ee!'

The creature ducked as Baron Marackai ran towards it.

The Baron reached into the hole and pulled the creature out by its neck. 'Well, well, what have we here?' he said, screwing up his nose.

It was a little grey goblin. It was dirty and wrinkly and wriggled in the Baron's grasp. In its bony hand the goblin was clutching a small black bat.

'Don't hurt me,' the goblin pleaded, its fat snout twitching.

The Baron smiled, his face twisting like a rotten apple core. 'Spying are you, goblin?'

The goblin's white eyes blinked. 'Help!' it called.

'There's no one to help you here, you revolting little creature,' the Baron said. 'The RSPCB is miles away!'

The goblin looked down at its bat. 'What to do, little bat? What to do?' he muttered.

'Give that to me, goblin,' Baron Marackai ordered.

'No! Not my bat!'

The Baron reached for the bat in the goblin's hands. 'I SAID, GIVE IT TO ME!'

CHAPTER TWO

At the RSPCB, the Royal Society for the Prevention of Cruelty to Beasts, Ulf was riding his quad bike through the beast park. The sun was shining as he sped across the Great Grazing Grounds then up on to the bridge above the meat-eaters' enclosures. Beneath him, in brick-walled pens, carnivorous beasts looked up: a gorgon hissed, a long-haired minotaur snorted at him and an Egyptian scorpius rattled its tail.

Halfway along the bridge, Ulf stopped and looked over at a beast with the body of a giraffe and the head of a piranha. This was the giranha, the tallest of all the meat-eaters. Its head was as high as the bridge. It turned towards Ulf, gnashing its teeth.

Ulf reached into a feeding-sack on the back of his quad bike and picked out a frozen chicken. 'Lunchtime,' he called, throwing the chicken across to the giranha.

The beast lunged with its long neck and snapped the chicken out of the air. Ulf watched as it gobbled the chicken whole.

'You're going home today,' he told it. 'Orson's coming to fetch you.'

Ulf turned, hearing the trees part at the edge of the Dark Forest. Orson the giant came striding out with a thick rope looped over his shoulder. 'How is she?' the giant boomed.

'She's doing fine,' Ulf called.

Orson strode to the gate of the giranha's enclosure and slid its metal bolt. As the giant pulled the gate open, the giranha reared up on its hind legs. 'Woah there!' Orson said.

The giranha stomped its hooves into the ground, gouging out great chunks of earth. It started screeching.

'Easy girl,' Orson said, clipping a beast collar to the end of his rope. The giranha lunged for him with open jaws, and Orson clicked the collar around the beast's neck. He heaved on the rope with his powerful arms, bringing the giranha under control.

Orson was huge. He could handle any beast. He looked at Ulf on the bridge. 'Off you go.'

Ulf revved his bike engine, then rode down the end of the bridge waving another frozen chicken in the air. 'Here girl, come and get it,' he called.

The giranha swung its head round to watch him.

'That's it, Ulf,' Orson said. 'Now let her have it!'

Ulf threw the chicken into the air. Orson relaxed the rope and the giranha lunged from its enclosure, catching the chicken in its jaws.

Ulf held a third chicken over his head as he rode into the Dark Forest. 'Come and get your food,' he called.

He sped along the forest track and heard the

giranha stomping behind him, pushing through the trees. He threw the chicken over his head, then glanced back to see the beast snap the frozen bird from the branches. Orson gripped the rope tightly, stopping the giranha from charging. Ulf held up a fourth chicken and accelerated away, luring the beast through the forest.

A sparkle flew across the track in front of him. It was Tiana the fairy. 'Hello, Ulf,' she said.

'Mind out, Tiana,' Ulf called, swerving. 'The giranha's coming!'

Tiana was Ulf's friend and lived in the Dark Forest with the other fairies. She was gathering leaves to make an autumn cloak.

She darted behind a tree and peered out nervously as the giranha stomped past, spitting out chicken bones.

Ulf rode on round the swamp and through the bracken. He jumped his bike over fallen branches and skidded on wet leaves. He splashed through puddles, and mud flew up

from the quad bike's wheels, splattering his jeans and T-shirt. Then the trees thinned and he rode out into the afternoon sun. He heard the screech of the giranha as it came out of the forest behind him, followed by Orson.

The giant called to him: 'Tell Dr Fielding the giranha's ready to go!'

The RSPCB was a rescue centre for rare and endangered beasts. The giranha had been brought in three months earlier, suffering from a broken hind leg. Dr Fielding, the RSPCB vet, had inserted a metre-long metal rod into its thigh bone to mend it. Orson had helped the giranha get strong again by taking it swimming in the freshwater lake. Now it was fully recovered and ready to be released back into the wild.

Ulf sped along the edge of the freshwater lake and into the paddock. The jackalopes were leaping in the sunshine. He heard a griffin screech from the aviary and looked across to see it landing in the branches of an oak tree. Ulf placed his hairy feet onto the foot bars and stood up on his quad bike, twisting back the bike's throttle with his hairy hand.

Though he looked like a human boy, Ulf was *beast blood*. He was a werewolf, a morphing beast, and on the full moon he would change from boy to wolf. The RSPCB was his home.

'Open,' he called as he reached a gate at the top of the paddock. The voice-activated gate opened automatically and he rode into the yard, pulling up outside a large country mansion. This was Farraway Hall, the headquarters of the RSPCB. Ulf stood up on his bike seat and peered in an open window. 'Dr Fielding,' he called.

'One moment, Ulf.'

He could see Dr Fielding in her office. She was on the telephone, speaking into the handset: 'That's terrific news, Minister. Antarctic dragons are the only flightless dragons in existence. A preservation order is long overdue. Thank you.'

She put the phone down. 'What is it, Ulf?'

'Orson's bringing the giranha in,' Ulf told her.

'Excellent. The transporter's waiting. I'll meet you out the front.'

Ulf rode round to the forecourt at the front of Farraway Hall. Parked by the entrance gates was the tallest lorry he'd ever seen. Its back doors were open and a ramp led up inside. It had straw on the floor and a trough of water.

He heard the stomping of hooves coming round the side of the house. He looked back and saw the giranha, being held by Orson. 'Easy girl,' the giant said.

Ulf threw four frozen chickens into the back of the lorry. The giranha saw them and stomped up the ramp. It screeched, then snapped one of them from the straw.

'That's it, big friend,' Orson said to the beast. 'Eat it up.'

While the giranha munched the chicken, Orson attached harnessing straps around its body to keep it steady on the long journey ahead. He stepped down and closed the doors. 'Thanks, Ulf,' he said.

Dr Fielding came out from the house and went over to the lorry to speak to the driver in his cab. 'Look after her,' she said. 'She's a soppy old thing really.'

'I'll see she makes it back safely,' the driver replied, starting the lorry's engine.

Ulf jumped off his quad bike and opened the front gates. He watched as the lorry drove out, heading away up the long driveway. The giranha was going back to its home in the African jungle. Ulf felt glad. He imagined it roaming free, pushing through the jungle trees.

'Well done, everyone,' Dr Fielding said, as she bolted the gates shut. 'One giranha safely mended and returning to the wild.'

Ulf smiled then hopped back on to his quad bike and rode after Orson. The giant was striding across the yard, whistling. 'Do you need a hand with anything else?' Ulf asked.

'No thanks, Ulf. I've just got to give the sandwhale its scrub, then I'm done,' Orson said. He picked up a broom from beside the kit room and slipped it into his belt. 'You get yourself something to eat, Ulf,' the giant told him. 'You need to be strong for tomorrow.'

Tomorrow night Ulf's transformation would take place. The moon would be full and he'd change from boy to wolf.

While Orson headed towards the desert dome, Ulf parked his bike by the feedstore. He fetched a sausage from the meat fridge, and sat on the paddock gate, eating it. The Mexican jackalopes were leaping in the long grass. He heard the low bellow of the Mongolian armourpod from out on the Great Grazing Grounds, and from Sunset Mountain came the *hurroooooo* of Bigfoot.

All the beasts would one day leave and go back to their homes in the wild, he thought. Ulf wondered when it would be his turn. He'd lived at the RSPCB almost all his life, ever since he'd been brought in as a werecub.

Ulf saw a sparkle shooting high over the paddock. It was Tiana the fairy.

'Look, Ulf,' she called, pointing. She was flying towards Farraway Hall, following a little black bat.

'A messenger bat!' Ulf said, excitedly. He jumped off the gate and ran towards the house, watching the bat circle above the chimney pots. It perched on the nose of a stone gargoyle that was leaning from the rooftop.

Uh-oh, Ulf thought.

The gargoyle turned from stone to flesh. It reached up. 'Gotcha!' it said, cupping its hands around the little black bat.

'Leave it alone, Druce!' Tiana yelled.

Druce the gargoyle stuck his yellow tongue out at the fairy then scuttled down a drainpipe, clutching the bat.

'Drop it, Druce!' Ulf said, running over. 'It's a messenger bat.'

'Messagy bat,' Druce gurgled, jumping to the ground. 'Drucey caught it.' The gargoyle held the bat close to his chest and pulled an ugly face.

Just then, the side door of Farraway Hall

opened and Dr Fielding came out. 'What's all the noise?'

'A messenger bat's come in,' Ulf explained.

Dr Fielding looked at the gargoyle. 'Druce, give that to me,' she said.

The gargoyle's mouth drooped.

'Be good, Druce,' she warned, stepping over to him.

Druce opened his hands and Dr Fielding took the small black bat. 'Thank you.'

'Blurgh!' Druce replied, blowing a raspberry, then he scurried back up the drainpipe to the roof.

'Who's it from?' Ulf asked.

Dr Fielding held the bat, inspecting a small gold ring on its leg. Engraved on the ring was a code. 'Spotter NOR8,' Dr Fielding read.

Tucked into the ring was a scrap of paper. 'Ulf, could you check the message, please?'

While Dr Fielding held the bat, Ulf carefully pulled out the scrap of paper from the ring. He unrolled it. Scrawled on it was a single word: HELP!

CHAPTER THREE

'Who's spotter NOR8?' Ulf asked, following Dr Fielding as she carried the messenger bat into Farraway Hall.

'I'll have to check the spotters' database,' Dr Fielding said.

Spotters were voluntary members of the RSPCB stationed around the world. They were essential to the RSPCB's global operations, relaying data on beast activity in the wild.

Dr Fielding was hurrying down the corridor. Ulf ran after her, holding the message in his hand. 'Do you think it's an emergency?' he asked. All the message said was HELP!

'Hopefully it's nothing serious,' Dr Fielding replied, opening the door of the data room.

Ulf stuffed the message in his pocket as he went inside.

The data room was the hub of the RSPCB Spotter Network. Pinned to the walls were maps and letters, and photographs of beasts. There was a spotters' board where beast sightings were recorded, shelves stacked with reports, and a desk with a computer and a small bat-cage beside it.

Dr Fielding placed the messenger bat in the cage, then sat at the computer to check the spotters' database. She tapped in the code NOR8 and the computer began searching.

Ulf saw Tiana waving at the window. He opened it and she flew in and landed by the bat-cage.

'I'll feed it,' she said. With both hands the fairy prised the lid from a tin marked MESSENGER MEALS. She picked out a dried grasshopper and poked it through the bars of the cage.

While the bat nibbled, Ulf looked at the spotters' board, reading the spotter codes on recent beast sightings from around the world:

SPOTTER AUS129: Mermaid spotted in Sydney harbour, Australia.

SPOTTER GBR215: Demon sighted at Westminster Cathedral, England.

SPOTTER USA333: Nixies found nesting in cornfield in Delaware, Pennsylvania. First of the season!

SPOTTER NEP56: Yeti footprints seen near food stores at Mount Everest base-camp.

'That's odd,' Dr Fielding said.

Ulf turned to the computer screen. It said **SPOTTER INACTIVE**.

'It must be one of the old ones,' Dr Fielding said. She span her chair to face the door, then put her fingers in her mouth and whistled. A small hand-shaped beast came scuttling on its fingertips into the room. It ran up the leg of her desk and tapped its finger, awaiting instructions. It was the Helping Hand, a busy beast that helped Dr Fielding with the RSPCB paperwork. 'Can you see what we've got on NOR8?' Dr Fielding asked it.

The Helping Hand scuttled to a cupboard in the corner. It pulled open the door with its fingers, and bundles of paper fell out on to the floor. The cupboard was stuffed full. The Helping Hand began rifling through folders and notes. Ulf watched as it pulled out sheets of paper, tossing them to the side. Then it disappeared to the back of the cupboard and Ulf heard rustling. The Helping Hand was leafing through the very oldest of the spotter files – spotters who had not been in contact with the RSPCB since the database was computerized.

'Most of the older spotters are inactive now,' Dr Fielding explained.

The Helping Hand came scurrying out holding a tatty sheet of paper. It climbed on to the table and handed the paper to Dr Fielding.

'Thank you,' she said.

Ulf looked. She was holding a form, creased and yellowed with age, and filled in by hand with black ink. On the top of the form it said

RSPCB SPOTTER LICENCE and in the upper corner was the code NOR8. Stapled to the form was a black-and-white photograph.

'How peculiar,' Dr Fielding said. She showed the photograph to Ulf. It was of a beast with large white eyes, pointy ears and a fat snout. 'Spotter NOR8 is a goblin,' she said.

'A goblin!' Tiana cried, looking up from the bat-cage.

'What's strange about that?' Ulf asked.

'I've not heard of a goblin being a spotter before,' Dr Fielding told him. She read the form. 'Name: Gumball.'

'Goblins are revolting, Ulf,' Tiana said. 'They're dirty and smelly. And they steal things.'

Dr Fielding frowned at the fairy. 'Tiana, that's not nice.'

'Well, it's true,' the fairy said. 'Goblins shouldn't be allowed to be spotters.'

Dr Fielding continued reading. 'Stationed in Norway.'

'Norway?' Ulf asked.

'A place called Honeycomb Mountain.

That messenger bat's flown all the way across the sea.'

Dr Fielding typed **Honeycomb Mountain** into her computer, pulling up information from the database. 'Honeycomb Mountain is in the Jotunheim Range.'

A three-dimensional digital image of a mountain came up on the computer screen. It was riddled with holes and caves and a network of tunnels.

'It's a habitat for underground beasts,' she said.

Dr Fielding clicked on images of wraith spiders, elephant leeches, cave mantises, sword serpents and longtusk trolls.

'What do you think's happened there?' Ulf asked.

'I expect the goblin's just got stuck in a hole,' she said.

'Goblins are always poking their noses into places they're not meant to,' Tiana added.

Ulf watched as Dr Fielding plugged in a handheld GPRS tracker and downloaded the information from the computer.

'You're not *going* there, are you?' Tiana asked. 'It's only a goblin.'

'Even so, I should check it out,' Dr Fielding said. 'I'll take the helicopter.'

She pulled up a satellite map on the computer screen to check the weather. It was swirling with dark cloud. 'There's a storm over the ocean. It's blowing this way,' she said. 'I'll leave first thing in the morning, as soon as the sky's clear.'

'Can I come with you?' Ulf asked her. He'd never met a goblin before. Despite what Tiana had said, he thought he'd quite like to.

'It's okay, Orson will come with me,' Dr Fielding told him. She got up and stepped to the door. 'We won't be gone long.'

'But I might be able to help,' Ulf said.

'The wild's a dangerous place, Ulf,' Dr Fielding told him. 'Anyway, I need you to look after things here.' She left the room and headed off down the corridor.

Ulf felt disappointed. He never got to go on expeditions.

'Who on earth would make a goblin a spotter?' Tiana muttered. She was stroking the bat through the bars of the cage.

Ulf looked down at the Spotter Licence. He read the RSPCB oath printed on it:

"I do solemnly swear to preserve and protect the wild. From this day forth, I pledge my allegiance to beasts."

Under the oath was a signature scrawled in awkward handwriting:

Gumball

Below it was written:

Appointed by Professor J.E. Farraway

'It was Professor Farraway,' Ulf said. 'Professor Farraway made the goblin a spotter.'

'He must have been crazy,' Tiana muttered.

Ulf frowned at her.

Professor Farraway had lived at Farraway Hall a long time ago. He'd been the world's first cryptozoologist and the founder of the RSPCB.

Just then, Ulf heard moanings and groanings coming from upstairs. He rushed to the door of the data room and poked his head out.

'Where are you going?' Tiana asked.

'Listen. It's him, Tiana,' Ulf said. Professor Farraway's ghost now haunted the old library at Farraway Hall. 'Let's see what he wants.'

Ulf started running down the corridor to the staircase.

'But it's spooky up there,' Tiana called, flying after him. Ulf was climbing the stairs. 'Come back, Ulf,' she said.

Ulf looked down. The little fairy was perched on the banister. Her wing tips were quivering. 'You're not frightened are you?' Ulf asked.

'Of course I'm not,' the fairy replied, crossing her arms.

Ulf reached his hand down to her. 'Come on. There's nothing to be afraid of.'

Tiana held tightly to the hairs on Ulf's palm. 'Just promise me we'll stick together,' she said.

CHAPTER FOUR

Ulf headed up the stairs with Tiana in his hand. He crept along the Gallery of Science and through the Room of Curiosities, past RSPCB artefacts and equipment from early expeditions. He stopped at a door on the far wall, the entrance to the old library where the non-corporeal beasts lived: ghosts, ghouls and spectres. Moanings and groanings were coming from inside. 'Ready?' he asked Tiana.

But before she could reply, the door creaked open. In the gloom of the library, Ulf saw a glowing blue mist disappearing through cracks between the floorboards. In the corner of the room a screaming mouth vanished into the wall, and on the upper reading level three ghostly grey heads rose up through the ceiling.

Ulf could feel Tiana clinging to his finger as the moanings and groanings fell silent. From the darkness on the far side of the library, Ulf saw a candle floating towards him. Its flame was flickering, lighting up the bookshelves.

'Professor, is that you?' he asked.

The candle drifted past Ulf's side and he felt a cold chill as the Professor's ghost went straight through him.

'Where's he going?' Tiana whispered.

The candle floated out through the doorway into the Room of Curiosities, hovering over boxes and crates.

'Professor, come back,' Ulf called, stepping after him.

The candle weaved between glass cabinets and cases. It floated past a dragon's tethering chain on the wall, and the chain began rattling. It hovered over a jar of vampire teeth, and the teeth began chattering.

'What's he up to?' Tiana asked.

The candle was lighting up objects, drifting over tables and along display cabinets. The lids of trunks and chests opened and closed. Drawers slid out and cupboard doors swung open.

'I don't know,' Ulf said.

The candle drifted to the far corner of the room and settled on a table. From beneath the table an old canvas rucksack slid out.

Ulf stepped over to it and saw its straps unbuckling. Objects rose out of the rucksack: a shiny silver compass flew out and popped into Ulf's pocket; a climbing rope snaked up and coiled around his shoulder; a metal head torch floated up and strapped itself to his head.

'Professor, what are you doing?' Ulf asked.

Tiana looked at Ulf, giggling. 'You look like an explorer.'

Ulf watched as an old map floated from a pouch in the rucksack and unfolded in the air. The map was drawn by hand in black ink, and was stained and streaked with dirt. It showed underground tunnels. Ulf could see passages connecting caves and caverns. They were labelled in tiny handwriting: Spider's Larder, Troll Chamber, Leech Lair, Gumball's Grotto.

'Tiana, look!' he said. 'This is where the goblin's stationed.'

At the bottom of the map it said Honeycomb Mountain.

The map folded itself up, then drifted down and wedged into Ulf's pocket.

'Let's get out of here,' Tiana said, flying past the candle. 'This is creepy.'

'Wait a minute,' Ulf said. He could hear something rattling in the rucksack. The strap on its side pocket undid and a small red box floated out.

Ulf took hold of the box. Its lid opened and inside it he saw bullets.

He gasped.

'Put that down, Ulf!' Tiana cried.

Ulf dropped the box and it landed with a clatter, the bullets spilling out across the floor.

'Let's go now,' Tiana told him. 'Bullets are dangerous.'

But as Ulf began edging away, he felt the icy chill of the Professor's ghost sweep through him. The hairs on Ulf's neck stood on end. He looked down. The bullets were moving on the floor, rolling out from under tables and behind crates. They were sliding back into the box. The box lid closed and it floated back up into his hand.

'Put that down, Ulf,' Tiana pleaded.

'But I can't, Tiana. He won't let me.'

The box of bullets was being pressed into Ulf's palm. On its side he saw the words: **TITANIUM-TIPPED BEAST BULLETS**.

The candle flickered and went out.

CHAPTER FIVE

Ulf ran out of the Room of Curiosities and along the Gallery of Science. As he passed a picture on the wall, he caught a glimpse of his reflection in the glass. He stopped, seeing the rope around his shoulder and the head torch strapped to his head. He stared at the box of bullets in his hand.

'You should give those to Dr Fielding,' Tiana said, hovering in front of him.

'But what was the Professor doing, Tiana?'

The fairy tugged on Ulf's ear. 'He was just being spooky,' she said, flying to the staircase. 'Come on.'

Ulf followed the fairy downstairs and into

the yard. He saw Dr Fielding and Orson by the kit room, getting ready for their expedition to Honeycomb Mountain. The sun was starting to go down and dark clouds were blowing in from the sea.

'The storm's coming,' Tiana said, hovering in front of Ulf.

Ulf hardly noticed her. He was still thinking about what the Professor had shown him.

'Go on, give Dr Fielding those bullets,' Tiana said.

A cold gust of wind blew the fairy head over heels and she grabbed Ulf's T-shirt to steady herself. 'I'm going back to the forest.'

Tiana started flying across the yard, weaving in the wind. 'I'll see you in the morning,' she called, then she disappeared over the big beast barn.

Ulf ran to Dr Fielding, clutching the box of bullets.

'Where have you been, Ulf?' Dr Fielding asked, seeing him dressed like an explorer.

'In the Room of Curiosities,' Ulf told her.

Orson bent down to look at the rope around Ulf's shoulder and the head torch on his head. 'Been rummaging through the Professor's things, have you?'

The giant tapped the metal head torch with his finger. 'They don't make them like that any more.'

'I found these,' Ulf said, showing Dr Fielding the box of bullets.

Dr Fielding took the box from him. 'Ulf, what are you doing with bullets?' she asked.

'They were with the Professor's things,' Ulf explained.

She took a bullet from the box and inspected it closely. 'This is live ammunition, Ulf. It's extremely dangerous.'

The bullet was shiny and its tip was sharpened to a point.

'Why would the Professor have bullets?' Ulf asked her.

Dr Fielding furrowed her brow. 'I think he probably confiscated these from a beast hunt. They're beast-hunting bullets, Ulf.'

Orson knelt down to take a look. 'Nasty things,' he said. 'Only humans could invent something so horrible.'

'Humans?' Ulf asked.

'They used to hunt beasts for sport, Ulf,' the giant said. 'They used to—'

'Orson, that's enough,' Dr Fielding interrupted. She turned to Ulf. 'There are no beast hunts any more, Ulf. Professor Farraway helped pass a law many years ago making them illegal. It was a major victory for beast protection.'

Ulf watched as Dr Fielding put the box of bullets in her pocket. 'I shall destroy these at once,' she told him. 'And if you ever find anything like these again, don't touch them, just come and tell me.'

Dr Fielding gave Ulf a stern look, then headed back across the yard to the house.

Ulf saw Druce the gargoyle leering from the roof of Farraway Hall. The gargoyle stared down at Dr Fielding and pointed his fingers like a gun. 'Bang!' he called. 'Bang! Bang!'

Dr Fielding looked up and saw Druce giggling. 'That's not funny, Druce,' she said.

The gargoyle pulled an ugly face, then turned to stone as Dr Fielding opened the side door of Farraway Hall. She glanced back at Orson. 'We'll leave at dawn,' she called. 'You'll need your flying cable.' The giant gave a thumbs-up and Dr Fielding headed inside.

'I think she's cross with me,' Ulf said.

'No she's not, Ulf. She just worries about you,' Orson told him.

The giant opened the kit room door and reached in, gathering the kit for the expedition.

'Those bullets were with the Professor's things from Honeycomb Mountain,' Ulf said.

'I expect they got put up there by accident,' Orson replied. 'The Room of Curiosities is packed with old stuff from all over the place.'

Orson pulled out his flying cable. He was too big to fit in the helicopter so he flew beneath it, suspended on a long steel cable with a footstrap at its end. He reached in again and pulled out a huge vest made from woven metal.

'What's that?' Ulf asked, staring at it.

'It's my chainmail vest,' Orson replied. 'In case of trolls.' He held it up for Ulf to see. The metal was worn and dented. 'Dr Fielding says there are longtusk trolls at Honeycomb Mountain. They're the biggest trolls of all, Ulf. Their tusks can go right through you.'

Orson folded the vest, then reached in for Dr Fielding's rucksack and caving boots.

'Do you think something bad has happened at Honeycomb Mountain?' Ulf asked.

The giant stood up, holding the kit in his arms. 'Don't pay too much attention to what a goblin says, Ulf. They're always causing trouble. The last time I saw one, it was stealing my kettle.' He gave Ulf a wink, then strode off across the yard towards the helicopter. As he reached the forecourt he turned. 'Don't worry about a thing, Ulf,' he called. 'We'll be back before you know it.'

Ulf looked up at the evening sky.

Stormclouds were gathering overhead.

BEASTLY BUSINESS

CHAPTER SIX

As the sky darkened, Ulf headed down the side of the big beast barn towards a stone hut with bars on its window. This was his den. He stepped inside, taking the rope from his shoulder, then pulled off the head torch and took the map and compass from his pockets. The message from Gumball the spotter fell out in the straw and he sat down looking at it: HELP! he read.

Ulf was wondering what had happened to the goblin. No one seemed to like goblins very much. No one except Professor Farraway, anyway. He reached to the back of his den and from his secret hiding place took out a small black book. It was Professor Farraway's old notebook: *The Book of Beasts*. He began flicking through the pages, past jottings on tracking pixies and a step-by-step guide to demon dentistry. He saw a sketch of the boola monster, a diagram of a minotaur's skull and tips on how to bottle a poltergeist. He found a section on underground beasts and stopped at an entry headed GOBLINS. Ulf read:

Goblins are expert thieves. They watch from the shadows, waiting to steal a scrap of meat or a shiny jewel to brighten their caves. Nothing goes on underground that a goblin doesn't see. Considered dirty and untrustworthy, they are seldom liked, but be nice to a goblin and it will help you, for a goblin will never forget a friend.

Ulf felt the wind blowing through the bars of his window. It was dark outside and starting to rain. He gathered the Professor's things around him, and tucked his knees into his chest. He imagined the Professor long ago on his expedition to Honeycomb Mountain, exploring the tunnels and caves underground. Then he thought about the bullets in the rucksack. Why did the Professor give them to him?

Ulf heard a gurgling sound and the patter of feet scurrying across the roof of his den. The sky flashed with lightning, and he saw Druce's face appear upside-down at the door.

The gargoyle pointed his fingers at Ulf. 'Bang!'

Ulf jumped. 'What are you doing here, Druce?'

The gargoyle dropped down and scurried around the side of Ulf's den. 'Drucey goes a-hunting. Hunting little beasties,' Ulf heard him gurgle.

The gargoyle popped up at the window, grinning. He pointed his fingers through the bars. 'Bang! Bang!'

'Stop mucking about, Druce,' Ulf said.

Druce blew the end of his fingers like a gun. He leant in further, screwing up his ugly face. '*Ma-rrrrackai* hunted beasts.'

'What are you talking about, Druce?' Ulf asked. Hearing the name Marackai sent a chill down Ulf's spine.

'Bad Marackai,' Druce said.

The gargoyle put his little finger into his mouth and bit it. 'I bited him,' he said. 'I bited his finger off.'

The gargoyle giggled, then ran off, bounding through the rain back to Farraway Hall. Ulf could see him scampering up to the dark rooftop. The gargoyle was singing: 'He comes in the night with his gun and his knife. Run away, Fur Face, run for your life!'

Ulf lay down in the darkness, thinking about Marackai. Marackai was Professor Farraway's son and had once lived at Farraway Hall. He hated beasts, and had been vicious and cruel to them. He'd been sent away, but twice he'd tried to take Farraway Hall back for himself. Twice Ulf had defeated him.

Ulf tried to sleep, but he couldn't. He had a creepy feeling that something bad was happening at Honeycomb Mountain. He stayed awake all night listening to the storm, thinking about the message and the bullets. As the storm blew itself out and the first rays of dawn appeared in the sky, Ulf knew what he had to do. He had to go on the expedition. He had to find out what was wrong.

Ulf picked up the head torch from the straw and put it on. He stuffed the map and compass into his pockets and slung the rope over his shoulder, then he crept out of his den.

The rain had stopped and the clouds were clearing. In the half-light, he saw Orson's lantern glowing from across the beast park. The giant was on his way back from giving the beasts their early-morning feed. Ulf ran through the yard to the corner of the house and saw Dr Fielding loading her medical rucksack into the back of the helicopter.

He looked up at Druce asleep on the rooftop. 'Psst,' he said.

The gargoyle turned from stone to flesh as he woke up.

'Keep an eye on things here for me, Druce,' Ulf whispered.

The gargoyle scurried down the drainpipe. 'Where's Fur Face going?' he gurgled.

'To Honeycomb Mountain,' Ulf whispered. 'You're in charge now.'

Druce smiled. 'Drucey the boss!'

'Ssh,' Ulf said. He saw Dr Fielding climbing into the cockpit of the helicopter. She was checking the flight controls.

Ulf saw that the cargo hold was open. With no one looking, he dashed across the forecourt and jumped into the back of the helicopter. He scrambled behind the pile of kit.

'Ready to go!' Dr Fielding called.

Ulf heard Orson's footsteps coming round the side of the house. He stayed hidden behind the kit as the giant loaded a lantern into the back of the helicopter. The door slid shut. It was pitch dark in the cargo hold. Ulf switched on his head torch and the light shone on metal walls. There were no windows. Then from under Orson's chainmail vest, a sparkle flew out. It was Tiana the fairy.

'Tiana!' Ulf said, amazed. 'What are you doing here?'

Tiana hovered in the torchlight. She was wearing a warm red cloak made from a pleated sycamore leaf. 'You didn't think I'd let you go on an expedition without me, did you?'

'But how did you know I was coming?'

Tiana smiled. 'You're a werewolf. You're always up to something.'

Ulf heard Dr Fielding calling to Orson outside. Then suddenly the helicopter engine started and Ulf heard the blades beginning to turn. He felt the helicopter lift off the ground.

'We're off,' he said excitedly.

There was a clanking sound as Orson clipped his flying cable to the bottom of the helicopter, then a jolt as the giant was lifted into the air.

Ulf felt the helicopter surge forwards, carrying him away from Farraway Hall.

CHAPTER SEVEN

Baron Marackai stood behind the reception desk in an old hotel, counting a bundle of money. He looked up as the front door opened and a flurry of snowflakes blew into the lobby. A man stepped inside, dragging a suitcase. He was wearing a camouflage jacket and a cowboy hat. He stamped his snowy boots on the mat.

'Ah, Mr Armstrong,' the Baron said. 'Welcome to Loadem Lodge.'

'Howdy,' the man replied.

'You're just in time for morning coffee. The others are waiting. If you wouldn't mind paying in advance, I'll show you through.'

'How much does this thing cost?' the man asked, pulling a wad of bank notes from his pocket.

The Baron took *all* the money. 'That'll do nicely,' he said. Then he rang a little bell on the desk and Bone came lumbering into the lobby, wearing a small peaked cap.

'My porter will take your bags upstairs, Mr Armstrong,' Baron Marackai said. He handed Bone a key attached to a key-ring in the shape of a pistol. 'Room five,' the Baron said. Then he stepped out from behind the reception desk. 'Come and meet the others, Mr Armstrong.'

Baron Marackai led the man across the lobby and pushed open the double doors to an oak-panelled room. 'Can I offer you a drink?'

'Sure thing,' Mr Armstrong replied.

Blud shuffled over carrying a tray with two steaming cups of coffee.

Mr Armstrong took one and sipped it slowly, looking around the room.

Seated in leather armchairs around a roaring

log fire were three men and a woman. They were all wearing camouflage clothing and sipping hot coffee.

'Leave us now, Blud,' Baron Marackai said, taking a cup for himself. He stood beside the fireplace, facing the guests. 'And now for the introductions,' he said. 'Mr Armstrong, I'd like you to meet everyone. This is Herr Herman Pinkel.'

A man with a red face and a bulbous nose stood up and shook Mr Armstrong's hand. 'Sehr gut. Sehr gut,' Herr Herman Pinkel said.

The Baron gestured to a tall man with shiny hair tied in a ponytail. 'And this is Señor Pedro Pedroso.'

The man stood up and kissed Mr Armstrong on both cheeks. 'Encantado,' he said.

'And this is the delightful Lady Semolina,' the Baron continued.

A stern-looking woman with a curly moustache held out her hand.

Mr Armstrong took it and kissed it. 'Delighted,' he said. 'I think.'

'And this is Mr Zachariah D. Biggles.'

A big black man wearing dark sunglasses stood up. He towered over Mr Armstrong. 'You can call me Biggy.'

'Howdy y'all,' Mr Armstrong said. 'You can call me Chuck.'

'Take a seat please, Mr Armstrong,' Baron Marackai said.

Chuck Armstrong sat in a leather armchair and stretched his legs out in front of the fire.

'Firstly, let me welcome you all to Loadem Lodge,' Baron Marackai continued. 'It has always been my dream to reopen this marvellous hunting hideaway. As some of you may know, beast hunting is in my blood.'

'Bravo,' Lady Semolina said, twiddling her moustache.

'For too long beast hunts have been banned because some do-gooders think they are cruel,' the Baron told them.

'Down viz ze do-gooderz!' Herr Herman Pinkel said.

'But *I* say that hunting beasts is what humans are best at. It's as natural as starting fires and fighting wars. And this evening you lucky people will sample the thrills of the greatest beast-hunting range ever built — the Predatron!'

The guests clapped.

'Yee-ha!' Chuck Armstrong cheered.

Baron Marackai stepped over to a large table covered by a white sheet. 'Gentlemen, Lady Semolina, choose your fun!' he said.

He pulled back the sheet and the guests gasped. Underneath were five rifles with telescopic sights, a pair of pistols in leather holsters, a crossbow and longbow with quivers of arrows, a leather belt of knives, harpoon guns, hand grenades, a flame-thrower and boxes of titanium-tipped beast bullets.

'Olé!' Pedro Pedroso said.

'Tally-ho!' Lady Semolina said.

'When do we start?' Chuck Armstrong asked.

'All in good time,' Baron Marackai told him. 'We have smoked out the prey and it is being

prepared. We shall hunt it this evening.' He lifted his cup. 'TO THE THRILL OF THE KILL!'

The guests stood up, raising their cups to the Baron. 'The thrill of the kill!' they repeated.

The small man Blud shuffled in through the door and tugged on the Baron's fur coat.

'What is it, you horrible little twerp?' Baron Marackai asked.

'There's a helicopter coming, Sir,' Blud whispered. He led Baron Marackai to the window on the far side of the room and wiped the misted glass with his red rag. The Baron looked out into the snowy sky. In the distance was the outline of a white mountain. Above it a helicopter was coming in to land.

'Well, well, look who it is,' Baron Marackai said. 'Get the vehicles, Blud. You know what to do.'

BEASTLY BUSINESS

CHAPTER EIGHT

Ulf's ears popped. The RSPCB helicopter was descending. 'We're landing,' he whispered to Tiana. He felt a jolt as Orson stepped from the flying cable, then heard a clanking sound as the giant unclipped the cable from the base of the helicopter. A few seconds later the helicopter touched down with a bump. Its engine stopped and Ulf heard the blades slowing.

'Stay quiet,' he whispered to Tiana.

From outside came muffled voices. Dr Fielding and Orson were talking. The door to the cargo hold slid open and Ulf felt a rush of cold air. He could hear the wind whistling outside. He hid under an old tarpaulin sheet as Orson reached in to unload the kit. Ulf heard the giant dragging his chainmail vest out of the helicopter.

'Could you pass me my rucksack, please?' Dr Fielding asked. 'And I'll need my caving boots.'

'What's the plan?' Orson asked.

'We'll have a look underground, check on the beasts and see if we can find this goblin.'

The door to the cargo hold slid shut. Ulf heard Orson and Dr Fielding getting kitted up, then they headed away from the helicopter.

'Let's go,' he whispered to Tiana. Ulf pushed off the tarpaulin sheet and gently opened the door. He squinted. Outside, a blizzard was blowing. Snowflakes were swirling and everything was bright white. They were on a snowy mountain that was dotted with caves. He saw Dr Fielding and Orson fifty metres away, heading to a cave with rocks around its entrance that looked like dragons' teeth. Dr Fielding was holding her GPRS tracker in her hand, and had her rucksack over her shoulder.

'Ready, Tiana?' Ulf asked.

Tiana wrapped herself in her red sycamore cloak with just her wings sticking out. 'It's chilly,' she said, flying through the gap in the door. She shivered, dodging the snowflakes.

As Dr Fielding and Orson entered the cave, Ulf jumped out of the cargo hold. His bare feet sunk into the snow.

'Won't you be cold?' Tiana asked.

'I'll be fine,' Ulf said. He was nearing his transformation. His blood was warming up and the hair on his hands and feet was starting to thicken. Tonight the moon would be full and he'd change from boy to wolf.

He looped the climbing rope over his shoulder, then headed across the snowy mountain towards the cave. He waited at the entrance, peering inside. At the back of the cave, a long dark tunnel sloped gradually downwards. He could see Orson and Dr Fielding heading along it. The giant was stooping, holding his lantern to light the way.

Ulf crept in, heading after them. 'Come on,

Tiana,' he whispered. Tiana flew beside him, glowing softly. They could hear the chittering sounds of underground beasts. Tiny eyes on stalks were peering from cracks in the walls.

'Friggs,' Ulf whispered. Frog-like beasts were watching them. Ulf trod carefully, feeling damp cold rock under his bare feet. Up ahead, Dr Fielding and Orson turned a corner, their lamplight slowly fading.

From the darkness, Ulf heard Dr Fielding calling, 'Gumball, are you here? It's the RSPCB-B-B.' Her voice echoed underground.

'The goblin's probably busy thieving,' Tiana said sharply.

'Ssh,' Ulf told her. 'If Dr Fielding finds out we're here, we'll be in big trouble.'

They crept round the corner at the end of the tunnel, but there was no sign of the light from Orson's lantern. Ulf switched on his head torch. He saw that the tunnel divided. Two passages led away in different directions.

'Which way did they go?' Tiana asked.

Ulf heard a noise from one of the passages. It

sounded like footsteps. 'Down here, Tiana,' he said, heading deeper into the mountain. The passage twisted and turned. As they crept along it, the sounds grew louder.

'Those aren't footsteps,' Tiana said.

Ulf listened. The sound was like daggers stabbing rock. He tiptoed into the darkness and the beam from his head torch shone down the passage, illuminating a large insect-like beast.

'Uh-oh,' Ulf said. Up ahead, stalking towards them along the tunnel, was a white beast with long articulated legs and two whip-like antennae. 'It's a cave mantis,' he whispered.

'Let's get out of here,' Tiana said.

'Just keep still. They're blind. It can't see us.'

The beast's eyelids were grown over. It was using its antennae to feel its way along the walls.

Ulf pressed his back against the side of the tunnel, and Tiana perched on his head torch.

'Stop fidgeting,' Ulf whispered.

'I'm not fidgeting.'

Ulf could hear something wriggling above him. A small lizard dropped down on to his

shoulder. He felt its foot tickling his ear. Ulf tried not to move.

He watched as the cave mantis approached, its antennae twitching. The beast stopped beside him. It was more than twice Ulf's height and its pale skin was so thin that he could see its heart beating and its belly full of toads and rats.

The lizard on Ulf's shoulder flicked out its forked tongue, licking his cheek, but he didn't dare flinch. He held his breath, staying completely still.

The cave mantis' antennae were feeling up the wall. The end of one antenna brushed over Ulf's neck. Suddenly, the cave mantis lifted its dagger-like leg, ready to strike. Ulf stayed frozen to the spot. The lizard started nibbling his ear. The cave mantis lunged, skewering the lizard against the rock.

Ulf kept still as the beast gobbled the lizard up then stalked away down the tunnel. Ulf breathed out. 'That was close,' he said.

Tiana flew into the air. 'Poor lizard.'

She flew down the tunnel, sparkling. 'Where did Dr Fielding and Orson go?'

'They've probably gone to look for the goblin,' Ulf said. He felt in his pocket and pulled out Professor Farraway's map. He unfolded it and, in the light from his head torch, traced his finger to the small cave labelled Gumball's Grotto.

'Well, which way is it?' Tiana asked.

Ulf looked carefully. 'I think we came in here,' he said, pointing to a jagged cavemouth. 'And the grotto's there.' He moved his finger. 'So that's down and west.'

He took the silver compass from his pocket, and checked which way the needle was pointing. 'West is this way,' he said, turning down a side tunnel.

He headed into a large underground chamber. Hanging from its ceiling were what looked like long spears of rock. There were hundreds of them, speckled in all different colours. They glistened in the light of Tiana's sparkles.

'They're beautiful,' Tiana said, weaving between them.

'Mind out, those are elephant leeches,' Ulf told her.

The spears of rock began rippling and swaying like the trunks of elephants, long leeches with fleshy suckers at their tips. They were reaching for Ulf and Tiana. One of them clamped on to Ulf's shoulder.

'No you don't,' Ulf said. He pulled the leech's sucker from his T-shirt, then he moved the leech aside and stepped past it. 'They're thirsty.'

Tiana weaved nervously among them as they coiled and turned towards her. 'I think they like my cloak,' she said.

'That's because it's red,' Ulf told her. 'The colour of blood.'

Tiana screamed and shot off through the chamber. Ulf pushed after her. 'They can suck more blood than a vampire,' he said. He was kicking through skin and bones on the ground.

At the far end of the chamber he stepped out into a tunnel.

He heard a faint echo: '—ball-all-all.'

'Listen, it's Dr Fielding,' Ulf whispered.

Her voice was coming from down the tunnel. 'Gumball, where are you-oo-oo?' Dr Fielding called.

Ulf and Tiana hurried towards the sound but the tunnel came to a dead end.

'Where is she?' Tiana asked.

'Gumball-all-all,' they heard again.

'It sounds like she's behind here,' Ulf said, pressing his ear to the wall at the end of the tunnel. The wall was warm and sticky, covered in a layer of mucus. He touched it with his hands. It was throbbing.

'That's not a wall. It's alive!' Tiana shrieked.

The wall was moving towards them. A hole opened in it, exposing a gummy mouth. It was a monstramaggot! It filled the width of the tunnel and was wriggling towards them.

'Eyugh!' Tiana said, darting back.

'Don't worry. It's perfectly harmless,' Ulf told her, wiping his slimy hand on his jeans. 'Monstramaggots only feed on bat poo.'

Tiana hovered in front of the enormous monstramaggot. 'It's revolting,' she said.

'We'll have to squeeze past it.'

'Yuck!' Tiana replied. She flew into the pocket of Ulf's jeans as he pressed himself against the side of the tunnel.

The monstramaggot began sliding past him, covering Ulf with slime. The slime soaked through Ulf's T-shirt and oozed down his jeans. The monstramaggot was a long one, six metres or more. Its sticky flesh rippled across his cheek, squishing him against the wall.

At last, with a slow sucking sound, the monstramaggot pushed past, and Ulf stepped back into the open tunnel behind it. His hair was clinging to his face. He shook his head and his hands, and slime flicked against the walls.

Tiana flew out of Ulf's pocket, shaking her delicate wings. They were dripping with monstramaggot mucus. She held her hand over her mouth, nearly vomiting. 'That was horrible,' she said.

Ulf wiped his head torch and looked down the tunnel. There was still no sign of Dr Fielding or Orson.

'Where did they go?' Tiana asked again.

'They must be nearby,' Ulf replied.

Tiana darted ahead, disappearing into an opening at the side of the tunnel. 'Look in here, Ulf,' she called.

Ulf ran to her, and saw the fairy hovering in a tall chamber.

'There are ropes in here,' she said. Tiana sparkled along a white rope that stretched across the chamber. 'Is this Gumball's Grotto?'

Ulf pulled out the Professor's map. By the light of his head torch, he found Leech Lair, then traced his finger along the tunnels.

'Ulf, look at this,' Tiana called.

Ulf looked over. The fairy was illuminating a dead owl wrapped in white rope. Ulf's head torch shone on another rope that ran vertically. He followed it up. It connected to another, then another. White silk ropes criss-crossed, stretching up to the ceiling. The dark cavern

hid a huge white web, and hanging in it were
dead owls, bats and shadowgulls.

Ulf looked again at the map. 'I don't think
this is Gumball's Grotto,' he said nervously.
'This looks like Spider's Larder.'

Tiana squealed.

Ulf looked up. Descending from the ceiling
on a rope of silk was an enormous wraith spider
with hairy legs a metre long. It was glowing
white with deadly venom. It dropped to the
ground, hissing, and its jaws opened, exposing
six mouths, each with razor-sharp fangs.

'Run!' Tiana screamed.

Ulf hurried through the chamber, clambering
through the white ropes as Tiana flew ahead.
They raced out the other side, then down a
long tunnel. They could hear the spider
scurrying after them.

Ulf ran as fast as he could.

'Hurry!' Tiana called.

Ahead, the beam from Ulf's head torch lit a
large opening in the side of the tunnel. 'In
there, Tiana! Hide!' Ulf called.

'Turn off your light!' Tiana said.

Ulf switched off his light and Tiana extinguished her sparkles so the spider couldn't see them. They dived through the large opening. It was pitch dark inside.

'Tiana?' Ulf whispered.

'I'm right here,' she said.

Ulf felt her wings fluttering against his cheek. He crouched low, hearing the spider coming up the tunnel. He could just make out its glowing white shape as it scurried past.

'Phew,' Tiana said.

As Tiana spoke, Ulf heard the spider stop.

For a moment there was silence.

Tap-tap-tap-tap. Tap-tap-tap-tap. The spider was coming back along the tunnel.

Ulf saw a hairy leg step through the opening. 'Oh dear,' he whispered.

The spider hissed. Then Ulf heard a loud grunting sound behind him and the spider quickly retreated. It scurried back down the tunnel.

'We're safe,' Tiana said.

'What was that noise?' Ulf whispered.

From behind them, in the dark, came another grunt then a low snuffling.

'It smells in here,' Tiana said.

Ulf sniffed. It did smell, of old meat and beast dung. He switched on his head torch and Tiana turned on her sparkles.

They were crouched in a vast underground chamber, bigger than a barn and twice as high. **All around them, staring from the shadows, were huge green trolls.**

BEASTLY BUSINESS

CHAPTER NINE

'Run!' Tiana said.

Ulf jumped to his feet, but the exit was blocked by an enormous male troll. More trolls were gathering on all sides. 'We're trapped, Tiana,' he said.

They were surrounded by over twenty trolls, the biggest Ulf had ever seen, with hairy chins and long tusks that grew from their lower lips.

'They look hungry,' Tiana said.

The trolls were edging nearer, drooling and slobbering, dragging their knuckles along the ground.

Some began growling. Others stood upright beating their chests. 'Oof! Oof! Oof!'

All around Ulf and Tiana, the trolls were closing in. One lunged at Tiana, swiping with its huge clawed hand. Tiana darted back.

Ulf heard a growl behind him. He swung round and saw a troll lumbering towards him, its huge tusks ready to strike. His head torch shone in its face and the troll stopped, holding its arm up to shield its eyes.

'They don't like the light,' Ulf said. He swung his head torch from one troll to the next. Tiana started flying in circles around him, glowing brightly, trying to keep the trolls away. But as each troll stepped back, another edged forward. 'Oof! Oof! Oof! Oof!'

Saliva was dribbling down their chins.

'Help!' Tiana screamed. 'They're going to eat us!'

Just then, Ulf heard loud thumping footsteps. He looked across to one of the tunnels coming off the chamber and saw lantern light.

It was Orson! The giant was running towards them.

'Orson! In here!' Ulf called.

Orson the giant burst into the Troll Chamber, his lantern held in front of him.

The trolls turned and growled.

'Help!' Tiana cried, flying up.

'Over here!' Ulf called from behind the trolls.

'Ulf! Tiana! Is that you?' Orson asked, peering over the trolls' heads. 'What are you doing here?'

One of the trolls charged at the giant. Its tusks clattered against Orson's chainmail vest. The giant stood firm and the troll charged again. Orson gripped one of its tusks, pushing the troll backwards.

The troll was fierce and strong, but it was no match for Orson.

The giant let the troll go, then turned up the gas on his lantern. The light grew brighter and all the trolls started backing away. 'They're beauties, aren't they, Ulf?' Orson said, striding further inside, swinging the lantern. 'That's it. Back you go,' he told the trolls.

Ulf watched as the trolls retreated to the edges of the chamber.

'You don't want to get caught by hungry longtusks,' Orson told him.

Ulf heard more footsteps as Dr Fielding came running down the tunnel shining a torch. She stopped at the entrance to the chamber. 'Ulf? Tiana?' she said. She marched in.

'You're in trouble now,' Orson whispered. He was swinging his lantern to keep the trolls back.

'What on earth are you two doing here?' Dr Fielding asked.

'It's my fault, Dr Fielding,' Ulf said. 'I wanted to come on the expedition.'

'But how did you get here?'

'In the back of the helicopter.'

Dr Fielding stared at Ulf in disbelief. 'It's not safe for you here.'

She shone her torch around the trolls. They were still grunting and growling.

'Sorry, Dr Fielding,' Ulf said, hanging his head.

Dr Fielding turned to the little fairy. 'And you should know better, Tiana.'

Tiana glowed with embarrassment. 'Sorry, Dr Fielding.'

Ulf stared at the ground. It was black. He bent down and wiped his hand over the chamber floor. It was covered in black dust. 'Look, Dr Fielding,' he said, showing her his hand.

Dr Fielding rubbed it. 'That's soot,' she said. She looked around the chamber. In the light of Orson's lantern, the walls looked black too. 'What's happened in here?' she asked.

She looked more closely at the trolls, taking care not to shine her torch in their eyes. Some of them had blackened skin. An adult female was scraping its sooty stomach. A wrinkled old troll with broken tusks was chewing a sooty bone. A male was grooming a female, trying to clean black soot from her back.

'Why are they sooty?' Ulf whispered.

Dr Fielding started walking very slowly towards the trolls. 'I don't know. It's odd.'

Orson held his lantern up to protect her. Ulf and Tiana followed.

As the trolls edged away from the light, Ulf noticed a big male lying on its side on the ground. A female was bent over the troll, licking its skin.

'That big one doesn't look well,' Tiana said, hovering close to Ulf.

Ulf took a step towards it.

The female troll turned and growled.

'Be careful,' Orson said. He swung his lantern from side to side and the female troll slowly backed away. 'That's it, girl. Give us a little space.'

Dr Fielding stepped to the big male troll lying on the ground. 'Stand guard please, Orson. I need to inspect it.'

While the giant stood over the troll with his lantern raised, Dr Fielding knelt down beside it. The troll wasn't moving.

Ulf watched. 'Is it alive?' he asked.

Tiana perched on the troll's shoulder. 'It's still warm.'

'Help me roll it over, Ulf,' Dr Fielding said.

Ulf and Dr Fielding gripped the troll's tusks and heaved, rolling it on to its back.

Dr Fielding pressed her ear to the troll's mouth and listened. 'It's only just breathing,' she said. She lifted the troll's wrinkled eyelids. Its eyes were cloudy. 'It's barely conscious.'

The troll coughed, and sticky black phlegm splattered its hairy chin.

Dr Fielding took off her rucksack and pulled out a packet of cotton wool. She wiped the black phlegm from its lips. With both hands she prised open the troll's mouth, then shone her torch inside.

'Urgh,' Tiana said, smelling the troll's breath. Ulf sniffed. It stank.

He stared at the troll's teeth. They were crooked and chipped, with bits of meat and fur stuck between them. Its tongue was thick and pitted. Its whole mouth was black with soot.

'It looks as if it has inhaled smoke,' Dr Fielding said.

'Smoke?' Ulf asked.

'See how swollen its throat is.'

Ulf looked to the back of the troll's mouth. The opening to its windpipe was constricted and its breathing sounded strained.

The troll snorted and more black phlegm leaked from its nose.

Dr Fielding handed the cotton wool to Ulf. 'Clean that up while I check its lungs,' she said.

Ulf started wiping the troll's nose. He put his finger up its nostrils, trying to clear its airways. The hairs inside the troll's nose felt bristly as he scooped out lumps of black gunk.

Dr Fielding held her stethoscope to the troll's chest and listened. 'Its lungs sound blocked,' she said.

The troll coughed. Then, as it tried to breathe in, it choked.

'What's happening?' Ulf asked.

The troll wheezed, then stopped breathing altogether.

'It's in respiratory arrest!' Dr Fielding said.

The troll lay still, as if it were dead.

Dr Fielding felt its wrist, checking for a pulse. 'Its heart's stopped. Stand back, Ulf.'

Ulf stepped back and watched as Dr Fielding placed both hands on the centre of the troll's broad green chest. She interlocked her fingers and, with her arms straight, started pressing down hard, again and again.

'What are you doing?' Ulf asked.

'Cardiopulmonary resuscitation,' Dr Fielding explained. 'CPR. We've got to get its heart and lungs working.'

She quickly placed her hand under the troll's hairy chin and tilted its head back to open its windpipe. Then she covered the troll's nose with both hands and took a deep breath.

Ulf watched as Dr Fielding opened her mouth and leant forwards, pressing her mouth over the troll's rubbery lips.

'Eyugh!' Tiana said, looking away. 'She's kissing the troll!'

Dr Fielding steadily breathed out into the troll's mouth.

'She's trying to help it breathe,' Ulf said.

Dr Fielding sat up and pushed the troll's chest again. It still wasn't moving. She took another breath and placed her mouth over the troll's, breathing air into it.

'Come on, troll. You can do it,' Ulf said.

Dr Fielding blew once more into the troll's mouth.

Suddenly, the troll coughed and its body convulsed.

Dr Fielding pulled her head away, wiping her lips.

The troll coughed again, splattering thick black phlegm over its tusks. It shook its head. It was breathing!

Dr Fielding took a bottle and a syringe from her rucksack. She quickly gave the troll an injection of adrenaline.

The troll grunted and licked its tusks, then rolled on to all fours.

'Move back, everyone,' Dr Fielding said.

Huddled under Orson's lantern, they all stepped away from the injured troll. As they did so, the female troll lumbered back over.

The two beasts touched tusks and snorted.

'What do you think happened to it?' Ulf asked.

Dr Fielding looked around. 'There's been a fire down here,' she said.

'A fire? Underground?'

Orson leant down, frowning in the lamplight. 'Fires don't just start by themselves.'

★　★　★

As the snow fell on Honeycomb Mountain, a cattle truck and an oil tanker wound their way up the icy track. They stopped near the top where the track finished.

The door of the oil tanker opened and Bone climbed down into the snow. From the side of the oil tanker he began unreeling a long hose.

Blud jumped out of the cattle truck with his rifle slung over his back. He glanced towards the RSPCB helicopter parked on the mountain. 'Deal with that, Bone,' he said.

The big man trudged to the helicopter and bent its blades with a metal hook.

Blud clambered to the oily hole at the top of the mountain. 'The RSPCB are doomed,' he sniggered, wiping his runny nose with a snotty red rag.

Bone dragged the hose from the oil tanker and headed after him. 'I always have to do the heavy work,' the big man grumbled.

Blud took the rifle from his shoulder. 'You're the oil man, I'm the shooter. If you've got a problem with that, talk to the Baron.'

Bone shoved the hose down the hole. He turned the nozzle on. There was a gurgling sound as thick black oil gushed from its end, pumping into the mountain.

Blud took a box of matches from his pocket. 'Time to warm them up.'

CHAPTER TEN

Dr Fielding shone her torch around the trolls. 'No other serious injuries,' she said.

Ulf was beside her. He felt a drip on his head and looked up. Another drip fell, then another. All around, drips began splashing on to the floor of the Troll Chamber. It was as if it was beginning to rain deep inside the mountain. He wiped his hair. Black liquid clung to his fingers. 'What's happening?' he asked.

Dr Fielding shone her torch on the roof of the chamber. 'It looks like oil,' she said.

Ulf could hear it trickling down the walls.

'Where's it coming from?' Orson asked.

Trolls started beating their chests. 'Oof! Oof! Oof! Oof!'

Some banged the walls with their fists.

As more oil poured down from the roof of the chamber, Tiana darted into Ulf's pocket to protect herself.

Suddenly, there was a roaring sound as the oil caught fire. Flames swirled around the ceiling and spread down the walls.

'Take cover!' Orson yelled. He threw his arms around Dr Fielding and Ulf, shielding them as flaming oil splashed to the ground.

The trolls charged for the exits.

The chamber was filling with smoke – thick, black smoke that made Ulf's eyes sting and bit into the back of his throat. He pulled his T-shirt up over his mouth.

'Get out!' Orson shouted. 'I'll get the trolls.'

Ulf tried to run, but in the thick smoke he could hardly see. He was coughing and choking. Flames were roaring around him. Trolls were crashing past him, barging him to the side as they raced to escape.

'Ulf! Over here,' he heard.

Ulf caught a glimpse of Dr Fielding's torch and staggered towards it. But at that moment, a sheet of flames fell in front of him. He shielded his face from the fire. 'It's no use!' he called. He was being pushed back by the heat.

A troll thumped into him and Ulf was knocked to the ground.

'Get up, Ulf,' Tiana called from his pocket.

He scrambled to his feet and staggered to the back of the burning chamber, following a group of stampeding trolls into a narrow exit. He'd lost Orson and Dr Fielding.

'We've got to get outside,' Tiana called. 'Run!'

Ulf ran as fast as he could up a back tunnel, slipping and sliding over the rocks. He heard a blast and glanced back as the chamber erupted in a fireball behind him.

The fireball hurled him through the air, and he landed with a thump, his head crashing against the tunnel wall. The lamp on his head torch smashed.

'Ulf, are you okay?' he heard from his pocket.

But everything was a blur. The bang to Ulf's head had injured him. He felt dizzy.

Then he felt his ankle being gripped by a bony hand. He was being dragged along the floor of the tunnel, and pulled into a cool dark cave. He heard a boulder being rolled across the entrance, cutting off the smoke.

Ulf felt himself losing consciousness. Tiana flew from his pocket, and in her glow he could just make out the face of a beast with white eyes, pointy ears and a fat snout.

A goblin was leaning over him.

'Gumball!' Ulf managed to say. Then everything went black.

BEASTLY BUSINESS

CHAPTER ELEVEN

Ulf opened his eyes. He was lying on his back, staring up at the roof of a cave. He sniffed. The cave smelt musty. He felt his head. There was a big bump on his scalp.

'Give that back!' he heard.

Ulf sat up and coughed. His mouth tasted of smoke. At the back of the cave, he saw Tiana's light. She was buzzing angrily above Gumball. The goblin was in the shadows, his bony hands clutching Ulf's broken head torch.

'Mine now,' the goblin said. 'My shiny.'

'It's not yours,' Tiana said indignantly. She pulled the strap of the head torch as hard as she could. 'It's Ulf's.'

'Tiana, what's going on?' Ulf asked.

Tiana glanced over at him. 'Ulf, you're awake! You've been out for hours,' she told him.

At that moment, the goblin yanked the strap of the head torch from Tiana's grip. 'Bad luck, fairy,' he told her. 'My shiny now.'

Ulf looked around. He was in Gumball's Grotto. By the light of Tiana's sparkles, he could see shiny metal objects dotting the walls: tin cans, bottle tops and coins.

'Let him have it, Tiana. It's broken anyway,' Ulf said.

'But he's a thief,' Tiana replied.

'He saved our lives,' Ulf told her.

'He only wanted your head torch.'

The goblin hugged the head torch and started polishing it against his chest. 'My shiny shiny,' he muttered.

'You're a selfish beast,' Tiana said to him.

The goblin looked across at Ulf and grinned. His teeth were black and broken, his face was dirty, and wispy grey hairs sprouted from his wrinkled skin.

'We've been looking for you, Gumball,' Ulf said. 'We got your message.'

'What message?' Gumball asked.

'Your messenger bat. It arrived yesterday.'

The little goblin smiled. 'My bat's safe?'

'It's at the RSPCB.'

The goblin stopped smiling and started trembling. 'I didn't send the messenger bat,' he said. Gumball stepped back into the shadows, clutching the head torch. '*He* did.'

'*He?*' Ulf asked, puzzled.

Gumball placed the head torch on a ledge on the wall, then started rearranging his shiny objects.

Tiana flew over and kicked a shiny tin can to the floor. 'Goblin, what are you talking about?'

The little goblin picked the can up and started polishing it.

'Who sent the messenger bat, Gumball?' Ulf asked.

The goblin's hand was shaking as he polished. 'Nasty man,' he said. 'Nasty man took my bat.'

'What nasty man?' Tiana asked.

The goblin raised his shaky hand and turned down his little finger. 'Nasty man missing finger.'

Ulf and Tiana gasped.

'Marackai!' Ulf said.

'Marackai's *here*?' Tiana shrieked.

'When did you see this man, Gumball?' Ulf asked.

'A day ago. Out there.' Gumball pointed to the ceiling.

Ulf looked up and saw a hole. He stepped to the wall and climbed up, poking his head into the hole. He felt cold air on his face. 'Come on, Tiana.'

Ulf squeezed through the hole and began pulling himself up a long craggy shaft, gripping hold of its rocky sides.

'Where are you going, Ulf?' Tiana called, flying after him.

'We have to warn Dr Fielding,' he called to her. He climbed higher and higher until he saw a layer of snow above him. He pushed up through the snow into bright daylight. Ulf squinted, wiping the snow from his head. He was at the top of Honeycomb Mountain. The blizzard had stopped and the sky was clearing.

Ulf climbed out and saw trolls lying on the ground. Tiana flew out behind him.

'What's happened?' she asked.

Ulf rushed to a troll and found a feathered dart stuck into its arm. It was snoring. 'They've been tranquillized,' he said, puzzled.

Ulf saw bootprints in the snow where humans had been walking. He traced them to a hole that was black and oily. On the ground was a matchbox. He picked it up. 'That fire was started on purpose!' he said.

Just then, Gumball the goblin poked his head out from his hole. 'Nasty man smoked out the trolls,' the little goblin said. 'He took the young ones away.'

'Ulf, look!' Tiana called. She was hovering over a rucksack that was half buried in the snow. It was Dr Fielding's. Orson's lantern lay smashed a short distance away. Ulf ran over and saw a crater in the snow the size of the giant and a long trench running to an icy track as if Orson had been dragged away. Ulf could see tyre marks on the track that led down the mountain. He looked across at the RSPCB helicopter. Its blades had been bent.

'Tiana, it was a trap!' he said. 'Marackai sent that message. And now he's taken Dr Fielding and Orson!'

'Taken them?' Tiana asked. 'Where?'

Ulf turned to the little goblin. 'Gumball, did you see where the nasty man went?' he asked.

'Bad place,' Gumball muttered.

'Gumball, we need to know,' Ulf said.

Gumball scurried over and tapped the matchbox in Ulf's hand. Ulf looked at it. On the matchbox was a picture of a wooden building. 'Loadem Lodge,' he read.

The goblin scuttled to the edge of the mountain.

'Where are you going?' Ulf called, running after him. Ulf stopped suddenly. It was a sheer drop down.

Gumball pointed north to the far end of a long valley. In the distance, Ulf could just make out a wooden building at the base of a hill. A thin trail of smoke was rising from its chimney…

★   ★   ★

In the hunter's lounge of Loadem Lodge, Baron Marackai was standing at the fireplace, a log fire crackling behind him as he finished telling a story. 'And that's how I bagged my first troll,' he said, smiling.

The guests cheered.

'Awesome!' Chuck Armstrong said.

'Tell us another one,' Lady Semolina said.

Baron Marackai fetched a large leatherbound photograph album from a cabinet at the side of the room. 'You'll enjoy this,' he said, laying it on a coffee table in front of his guests.

The guests turned the pages of the photograph album one at a time, their eyes wide with excitement.

'Those were the days,' Baron Marackai said. 'Oh, to have lived then!'

The album was full of old black-and-white photographs of beast hunters, each proudly holding up the head of a dead beast mounted on a plaque.

'Now *zat* iz vot I call hunting,' Herr Herman Pinkel said.

'Those guys were real experts,' Chuck Armstrong added.

'Great men, all of them,' the Baron said. '*Real* men.'

He gave Lady Semolina a wink. She giggled and licked her moustache.

Then the door opened. The Baron looked round as Blud stepped in. 'What is it, Blud? Can't you see I'm enthralling these people with my stories?'

'It's all done, Sir,' Blud told him.

'Splendid,' the Baron replied, ushering the small man back out into the lobby. He closed the door behind him. 'Were they all there?' he asked.

'No, Sir,' Blud replied. 'Just the vet and the giant.'

'Are you certain?'

'Yes, Sir.'

'Oh, what a shame,' the Baron sighed. 'I had hoped the werewolf would come too. It's a full moon tonight. I wanted his beast head for my wall.'

Blud sneezed, then wiped his nose with his snotty red rag. 'What shall we do with the prisoners? Can we kill them now?'

'Not yet,' the Baron told him. 'I have plans for them. We're going to have a little fun tonight!'

CHAPTER TWELVE

'Come on, Ulf. We have to get to Loadem Lodge,' Tiana called, flying towards the long winding track that led down the mountain.

Ulf unfolded Professor Farraway's map. 'Wait a second,' he told her. On the map was a long hollow shaft that spiralled down through the centre of the mountain. The Corkscrew, he read. 'There's a quicker way.'

Ulf took the silver compass from his pocket to check his bearings.

The little goblin reached out and touched the compass. 'Shiny,' he said.

Tiana came flying back. 'You're not having that, Gumball,' she said.

'Sorry, Gumball, I need this,' Ulf told him, checking which way the compass needle was pointing. He looked at the little goblin. Gumball's eyes were fixed on the shiny silver.

'Thanks for your help,' Ulf said. 'But I'm afraid we have to go now.'

Ulf turned and ran off through the snow, looking for a square-sided cave. 'In here, Tiana,' he called.

Tiana flew over and darted after Ulf into the cave. Her sparkles illuminated the walls.

Ulf navigated using the Professor's map. He squeezed along narrow passageways and ducked through openings. Every so often he heard the sound of little footsteps behind him.

Gumball was following.

'What's he doing?' Ulf asked.

'He wants your compass,' Tiana said.

'Maybe he just wants to help,' Ulf told her.

Ulf stopped and glanced back up the tunnel. The goblin scurried behind a rock.

'Gumball!' Ulf called. 'It's okay. You can come with us.'

Gumball was hiding.

'Goblins are so shifty,' Tiana said. 'Come on, leave him.'

Ulf turned and continued down the tunnel. He led the way to a round chamber with damp walls. In its centre was a large hole in the floor. Water was trickling into it.

'Are you sure this is the way?' Tiana asked.

'It says so on the Professor's map,' Ulf replied. He peered down the hole. It fell away into blackness. He picked up a stone and dropped it down. He heard it clattering against rock, counting to twenty as the sounds became fainter. 'This must be the Corkscrew.'

'It sounds a long way down,' Tiana said. 'Are you sure it's safe?'

'We have to hurry,' Ulf replied. He slipped the map and compass into his pockets, then sat on the edge of the hole. 'See you at the bottom.'

Ulf dropped feet-first into the hole and shot downwards, sliding against the wet walls of a narrow shaft. Water sprayed into his eyes and mouth and a *whooshing* sound roared in his ears as he gathered speed. The shaft was pitch black. It twisted and turned round and round like a corkscrew. He was hurtling faster and faster down through the mountain.

Suddenly, he felt the walls vanish. He was falling through air. Below, he could hear the roar of rushing water. He landed with a splash, plunging into an ice-cold underground river. Ulf sank, tumbling and twisting. He kicked his legs and swam to the surface.

'Are you okay?' he heard. He looked up and saw Tiana zooming down towards him, her sparkles illuminating the water. Ulf gasped. He was being swept away. He saw his map being washed downriver, and his rope uncoiling from his shoulder in the current. Ulf grabbed its end.

'Over here, Ulf,' Tiana called, flying to a rocky shore at the edge of the river. Ulf kicked frantically, swimming as hard as he could, fighting against the current. He reached for the rocks, grabbing hold of them, then pulled himself out. Behind him, he heard a splash.

'What was that?' he asked.

Tiana flew out across the water. By her light, Ulf saw pointy ears surface in the river.

'Oh no, it's Gumball,' Tiana cried.

The little goblin was struggling to stay afloat, his arms thrashing. 'Help!' he called. He was being dragged along by the current.

Downriver, Ulf saw a line of yellow fins rise from the water. He watched in horror as the huge head of a sword serpent broke the surface. 'Gumball, swim!' he called.

Tiana was flying above the little goblin. 'Gumball, swim, you idiot!' she yelled. 'You'll get eaten!'

The goblin was being washed towards the serpent.

'Gumball, watch out!' Ulf called.

The serpent opened its jaws, its fangs glinting like swords.

Quickly, Ulf tied a loop in his rope to make a lasso. He swung the lasso over his head, then threw it. The serpent lunged. The lasso looped around Gumball, and Ulf tugged. The serpent's jaws slammed shut, just missing the goblin. Ulf pulled on the rope as fast as he could, dragging Gumball through the water. The sword serpent thrashed its tail and followed. It hissed as Ulf heaved Gumball on to the rocks, then it butted the shore and disappeared back under the water. The soaking-wet goblin lay on the rocks, spluttering.

'Are you okay, Gumball?' Ulf asked.

'You silly beast,' Tiana said, darting over. 'You could have died.'

Gumball squirted water from his mouth. 'Gumball coming too,' he said.

Ulf smiled, then pulled out his compass, trying to work out which way to go next.

Gumball reached out his bony hand. 'Gimme,' he said to Ulf.

Tiana slapped the goblin's finger. 'You ungrateful beast,' she said. 'Is that stupid compass all you can think about? Ulf just saved your life.'

Gumball drew his hand back slowly.

'Come on,' Ulf said, slipping the compass safely back into his pocket. 'It's not far now.'

BEASTLY BUSINESS

CHAPTER THIRTEEN

Blud and Bone were at work in the dungeons below Loadem Lodge.

The big man Bone walked along a row of cages, throwing buckets of water through the bars.

In each cage a troll woke up and growled.

Blud reached into a wooden crate and pulled out a meaty steak. 'Dinner time,' he said, dangling it in front of the cages.

The trolls lumbered forwards, clattering their tusks against the metal bars. They grunted, reaching for the meat.

'They're hungry,' Bone said, grinning.

The trolls were drooling.

Blud wafted the meaty steak in front of them. 'Lovely juicy meat!' he said.

The trolls rammed the bars of the cages, snorting and slobbering.

'But you're not having it.'

Blud pulled the meat away and Bone laughed.

'They're starving,' Bone said.

'That's how the Baron wants them,' Blud told him.

From his jacket pocket Blud took out a large sewing needle and a ball of string. He grabbed lots more meaty steaks from the crate, then sat on the floor, stitching them all together.

'What are you doing?' Bone asked.

'You'll see,' Blud replied.

While Blud stitched, the trolls rattled the bars with their tusks. They were watching him, groaning with hunger.

Bone picked out the biggest, juiciest steak he could find. 'Can I eat one?' he asked.

'No!' Blud said. 'Give that here.'

When Blud had stitched together all the steaks from the crate, he held up a big blanket of meat.

'What's that for?' Bone asked.

'It's part of the Baron's plan,' Blud told him.

Blud carried the blanket of meat out of the dungeons, heading through a stone archway and along a corridor. Flaming torches lined the walls, lighting doors on either side. Bone watched as Blud carried the blanket of meat through a door marked BAIT ROOM. A moment later he came back out, grinning. He wiped his hands on his trousers.

'What have you done with it?' Bone asked.

'It's a surprise,' Blud said, tapping the side of his nose. 'You'll have to wait and see.' The small man stepped across the corridor to a door marked TROPHY PROCESSING ROOM. 'Come on. It's time to grease the guillotine.'

Both men stepped inside. In the centre of the room stood a tall contraption. This was the guillotine, a machine used to remove the heads of hunted beasts as trophies. It looked like a large metal bench with chains across it, and two steel uprights at one end. Between the uprights was a big metal blade.

Rats scurried across the room, sniffing around a basket on the floor at the end of the guillotine.

Blud kicked his way through the rats and jumped up on to the bench. 'Get the grease,' he said.

From a tub in the corner of the room, Bone scooped out a handful of grease. He rubbed the grease up and down the steel uprights.

'Let's try it,' Blud said. The small man took a meaty steak from his pocket and handed it to Bone. 'Stick this under the blade.' He pulled on a rope at the side of the guillotine and the big metal blade started lifting up.

Bone laid the meat on the end of the bench.

Rats started jumping up, trying to nibble it.

Blud was singing: '**YOU are the greaser. Grease, grease, grease. I am the chopper. Chop, chop, chop.**' He let go of the rope and the metal blade dropped between the uprights.

It thudded down, chopping the meat in two. A bloody chunk of steak fell into the basket on the floor. Rats scurried over, climbing into the basket to gobble the meat up.

'Blud! Bone!' they heard. 'Where are you?'

Footsteps were coming along the corridor outside. The door opened and Baron Marackai looked in. He saw the meat in the basket. 'You're not to play with the guillotine!' he shouted. 'We'll need that nice and sharp for after the hunt. We'll be making trophies from the trolls' heads.'

Blud jumped down from the bench. 'Sorry, Baron,' he said.

A rat scampered up Blud's trouser leg.

'Are the giant and the vet secure?' the Baron asked.

'Yes, Baron,' Blud said, hopping and wriggling. He shook his leg.

'Then it's time to prepare the Predatron. I want all the machines checked.'

Blud squealed as the rat nibbled.

'And stop messing around!'

BEASTLY
BUSINESS

CHAPTER FOURTEEN

With the sound of the river fading behind them, Ulf and Tiana crept down a narrow passageway. They came to a dead end.

'We're lost,' Tiana said.

Ulf took out his compass, checking his bearings.

Gumball crept beside him. 'Gumball help,' the goblin said.

Gumball reached out and tapped his bony knuckles against the wall. It sounded as if the wall was made of metal.

Ulf pushed against it and a sheet of rusty corrugated iron bent outwards. 'Thanks Gumball,' he said, ducking through.

He came out in a wide tunnel that was lit by a line of electric light bulbs.

Tiana flew after him. 'What is this place?' she asked.

The line of bulbs stretched in either direction, and railtracks ran along the ground. The tunnel was made of rusting iron. Ladders were bolted to the walls, leading up and down through hatches.

Gumball scurried to Ulf's side. 'Nasty here,' he muttered.

'What do you mean, Gumball?' Ulf asked.

'Professor shut it long time ago.'

'Professor Farraway?'

Gumball stepped into the light. 'Professor friend. Professor made me spotter,' he said proudly.

'I can't think why,' Tiana muttered. She flew off down the tunnel.

The little goblin looked at Ulf, grinning with his broken teeth. 'Gumball good spotter. I see everything.'

Ulf saw Gumball's eyes creeping towards his compass. He slipped it back in his pocket.

'Ulf, look at this,' Tiana called.

Ulf ran to look. The fairy was hovering by a contraption on a wrought-iron stand. It looked like a huge metal box with a large tube poking from it. It had a mechanism of springs, rubber belts and freshly-greased cogs. Inside the box, Ulf could see big black balls, and on its side was a lever. A sign read **STICKY STUCKY**.

'What is this, Gumball?' Ulf asked. He turned back. The goblin was creeping up behind him, reaching for his pocket.

Gumball quickly pulled his hand back and started biting his dirty fingernails. 'Hunters built the machines,' he mumbled. He pointed to a hatch in the wall that was bolted shut. 'They hunted beasts out there.'

Ulf slid the bolt sideways and swung the hatch open. Daylight flooded in as he looked across a wide snowy valley. In its middle, a tall metal pole was sticking out of the ground. Hanging from the top of the pole, on a chain, was a large metal ball.

Further down the valley, he could make out

the long metal arm of a crane. It was white with fresh snow, and on its end was a big mechanical claw.

On the ground by the crane, he saw the snow move. A hatch lifted open and a big man with a thick beard climbed out, carrying a pot and a shovel. Behind him came a small man dabbing his nose with a red rag.

'Look,' Ulf said.

It was the Baron's men.

'What are they doing?' Tiana asked, flying to Ulf's shoulder.

The big man began shovelling snow from the base of the crane. As he dug, Ulf heard a clang. It sounded like the ground beneath the snow was made of metal too.

Nearby, the small man poked the snow with a stick, and a large metal disc sprang up on a spring. 'Bone, here's one!' he called.

The big man trudged over carrying the pot. He dipped his hand in, scooping out a lump of grease. He greased the spring, then pushed the disc back under the snow.

Ulf looked along the valley. He saw metal pipes poking up from the snow. On the sides of the valley he could make out snowy balconies and spotlights. The valley was entirely man-made. 'I don't like the look of this, Tiana,' he said, closing the hatch. 'We should hurry.'

Ulf set off along the tunnel with Tiana flying after him. Beside the railtrack he found a four-wheeled cart turned upside down. Ulf turned the cart over.

'What are you doing, Ulf?' Tiana asked.

The cart had a wooden seat and pedals on the floor. Ulf lifted it on to the tracks and sat in it. 'We'll go faster in this,' he said.

He started pedalling and the cart began to move. Tiana perched on the front, holding on tightly as they picked up speed.

Gumball came running after them.

'Oh no, are you coming too, Gumball?' Tiana asked.

The goblin caught up and hopped in behind Ulf. 'Gumball be passenger,' he said.

As they rolled forwards, the tunnel widened. Above them, Ulf saw huge iron pistons stretching from one wall to the other. He pedalled past a sign saying **THE CRUSHER**.

The track weaved between girders, cables and pipes. It was as if they were inside the workings of a huge machine. Ulf pedalled harder. Up ahead the track divided. One route continued straight; the other looped left and downwards. The cart veered to the left.

Tiana shrieked as they whirled down.

Ulf lifted his feet. The pedals were spinning. 'This is more like it!' he called.

Tiana clung to the front of the cart, trying not to be blown away.

'We're going under the valley,' Ulf said.

The track twisted and turned and the cart sped down between dozens of metal columns. The columns rose from floor to ceiling. Ulf saw more tracks running off into the darkness as they shot past a sign saying **FOREST OF FEAR**. Above him, through metal grilles, Ulf could see snow.

The track weaved, then twisted upwards again. Ulf pedalled up a slope and the wheels squeaked. As he reached the top, the cart lurched round a bend and Ulf saw a sign saying **DROWNING POOL**.

Gumball stood up and leaned forwards. 'Wolfy pedal good,' he said.

'Sit down,' Ulf said. 'You'll fall out.'

Gumball wobbled and fell on to Ulf. 'Oopsy,' the goblin said, grinning. He sat back down as the track straightened.

They passed shelves full of boulders lined up above a metal chute. The chute was poking out into the valley. **SKITTLE ALLEY**, another sign read.

'Look, Ulf!' Tiana said, pointing ahead.

The track was coming to an end. Ulf saw empty pedal-carts parked in a circle. Beyond them was a big wooden door.

Gumball pulled a lever on the side of the cart and it squeaked to a halt. He hopped out and scuttled behind the pedal-carts. 'Loadem Lodge behind that door,' he said. 'Good luck.'

He was holding something in his hands.

'Hang on, what's that you've got?' Tiana asked suspiciously. She flew over to Gumball.

The little goblin was clutching Ulf's compass.

'Hey! Give that back, slimeball!' Tiana cried.

'Mine now,' Gumball said. 'My shiny.'

'Thief!' Tiana said. 'Ulf, he picked your pocket!'

Gumball clutched the compass to his chest.

Ulf climbed out of the pedal-cart. 'It's okay, Gumball, you can keep it now,' he told him.

'Keep?' Gumball asked.

'Yes,' Ulf replied.

Gumball stepped forwards. He was smiling. 'Friend,' he said, holding out his bony hand.

Ulf shook it. Gumball's hand felt cold and frail. 'Thank you for helping us get here,' Ulf said to him.

Tiana glowed furiously. 'But he stole it from you, Ulf!'

'We don't need it any more,' Ulf told her. 'Come on, it's time to save Dr Fielding and Orson.'

He stepped past the pedal-carts to the wooden door, then looked over his shoulder. 'Gumball, are you coming too?'

The little goblin was polishing the silver compass. 'No. I keep watch,' he muttered, stepping into the shadows.

'Oh, sure he will,' Tiana said, flying to Ulf's shoulder. 'He'll be off as soon as we're inside. He only came for your compass.'

The goblin's white eyes were blinking in the shadows. Ulf smiled, then he pushed the big wooden door open and stepped inside. He found himself in a stone corridor. Ulf glanced down a line of flaming torches lighting the walls. He could hear a voice coming from beyond a stone archway at the end of the corridor: 'AND THIS IS WHAT YOU'LL BE HUNTING!'

It was the voice of Baron Marackai...

CHAPTER FIFTEEN

Ulf crept along the flame-lit corridor past doors marked TROPHY PROCESSING ROOM, BAIT ROOM and ARMOURY. He stopped at the stone archway, hidden in the shadows. Tiana flew beside him and hovered above three levers sticking out from the wall.

They peered into what looked like dungeons. Standing less than ten metres away, with his back to them, was Baron Marackai. The Baron was dressed in a fur coat and serpent-skin boots. With him were five humans in camouflage clothing.

'Hunters,' Ulf whispered.

They were facing a row of cages. Inside

each cage a big green troll was snorting and grunting.

'As you can see,' Baron Marackai said, 'we have gathered only the finest specimens. Each of them is young and unblemished. Their heads will look splendid displayed on the walls of your homes.'

Baron Marackai led the hunters along the row of cages.

'Ven can ve kill zem?' a man with a red face asked.

'Not long now, Herr Pinkel. In just a few moments, I shall release these beasts into our magnificent hunting range where you can pursue them with weapons of your choice.'

'We no be in danger?' a man with a ponytail asked.

'Of course not, Señor Pedroso. I can assure you that these beasts do not stand a chance. Everything has been carefully designed to the hunter's advantage.'

At that moment, Ulf heard a clattering

sound from back down the corridor; a pedal-cart was pulling up in the tunnel.

'Quick, Ulf, hide,' Tiana whispered.

Ulf crawled quietly into the dungeons and hid behind a large wooden crate. It smelt of meat.

Tiana perched on his shoulder. They peered around the side of the crate as the Baron's men entered through the archway.

The Baron turned to the men. 'About time, too,' he said. 'Are the machines ready?'

'All oiled and greased, Sir,' Blud replied.

'Marvellous!'

The Baron faced the hunters. He smiled. 'Tonight marks our opening night, so I have prepared a special treat for you, a bonus prize for one lucky shooter.'

The Baron strode along the cages. At the end of the row was a cage draped in camouflage netting. He pulled the netting aside. 'Imagine that big head on your wall!'

The hunters gasped.

'A giant!' a big black man in sunglasses said.

'Not just any giant, Mr Biggles,' the Baron replied. 'This is the RSPCB's giant!'

Inside the cage, Ulf saw Orson lying on the floor unconscious.

Bone stepped across with a bucket of water and threw it over the giant.

Orson's eyes opened and he slowly sat up. 'What's going on?' he groaned.

'Welcome to Loadem Lodge,' the Baron said through the bars.

Orson stood up, hunched over. He was too big for the cage. He saw the trolls in the cages alongside him. 'What are they doing here?'

'The same as you, Mr Orson,' the Baron replied. 'Preparing to die.'

The hunters laughed.

A man in a cowboy hat pointed his finger like a gun. 'Pow! Pow! I'm gonna get that giant!'

'There's plenty of him to aim for, Mr Armstrong,' the Baron replied.

Orson shook the bars of his cage. 'Where's Dr Fielding?' he demanded.

Baron Marackai grinned. 'Oh, that reminds me. Blud, fetch the bait!'

Blud left the room, and a moment later Ulf heard an engine start. Blud rode back through the archway on a black motorbike, dragging Dr Fielding on a rope. She was being pulled along the stone floor.

'What has he done to her?' Tiana whispered in horror.

Dr Fielding's hands and feet were tied, her mouth was gagged with a crusty red rag and she was wrapped in a blanket of meaty steaks.

The trolls started grunting and drooling when they smelt the steaks. They clattered their tusks against the bars.

Baron Marackai was laughing. 'Oh, I do love your outfit, Dr Fielding,' he said, prodding one of the steaks with his finger.

'I'll crush you, Marackai,' Orson boomed from his cage.

The Baron turned. 'Empty threats in the circumstances, Mr Orson.'

He faced the hunters. 'Everyone, please do

show your appreciation for Dr Fielding, the RSPCB vet.'

'Boo! Hiss!' the hunters cried.

'Tonight, she will be our bait. We shall use her to lure the trolls to your guns.'

Dr Fielding lay wriggling on the floor, wrapped in the meat blanket and unable to stand.

The Baron raised his right hand. 'Death to the RSPCB!' he said.

The hunters held up their right hands and folded down their little fingers. 'Death to the RSPCB!'

Ulf clenched his fist.

'Ulf, don't do anything stupid,' Tiana warned.

'Hunters, it's time to begin the hunt!'

Ulf leapt over the crate. 'Stop!' he shouted, diving and knocking Baron Marackai to the floor.

'Werewolf!' the Baron cried. 'What are y—'

Ulf bashed him on the nose.

'Ouch! Bone, get him off me!'

Ulf felt a pair of strong hands dragging him

off. The big man threw Ulf to the floor, pinning him down with his boot.

'Well, well,' Baron Marackai said, standing up and rubbing his nose. 'So you decided to join us after all, werewolf.' He glanced to the hunters. 'I loathe werewolves,' he said.

A woman with a moustache peered down at Ulf. 'Can we hunt it?' she asked.

'Not this one, Lady Semolina,' Baron Marackai said. 'This beast's mine.'

Ulf was struggling beneath Bone's boot. It was pressed hard to his chest and he could barely breathe.

'Leave him alone or I'll tear your arms off!' Orson called through the bars of his cage.

Baron Marackai laughed. 'No you won't, Mr Orson. You're going in the Predatron where you'll be killed like any other beast. Hunters, fetch your weapons! BONE, BRING THE WEREWOLF TO THE PROCESSING ROOM!'

CHAPTER SIXTEEN

Ulf was carried, punching and struggling, down the stone corridor to a room that was writhing with rats.

'Lay him on the guillotine,' the Baron said.

Bone dumped Ulf on to a contraption in the middle of the room.

'Face up,' the Baron ordered.

Bone flipped Ulf on to his back, pressing him flat on a bench. Ulf scratched Bone's arm.

'Ow! Stop squirming, you little twerp.'

'Tie him,' Baron Marackai said. He stood at the end of the contraption and pulled on a rope.

The big man pushed Ulf's head out over

the end of the bench and began wrapping him in chains.

Ulf looked up.

As the Baron pulled the rope, a large metal blade was lifting high above Ulf's neck.

'You'll never get away with this,' Ulf said.

'Oh, but I will,' the Baron replied, grinning. 'The RSPCB is finished.'

Bone pulled the chains tight around Ulf's legs and arms. 'Can I do the chopping?' the big man asked.

'Not yet,' Baron Marackai said. 'I want his beast head.'

The blade was suspended above Ulf, ready to drop. The Baron tied the rope to a hook on the floor, then stepped to the wall and reached up, opening a high metal hatch. A cold wind blew in and Ulf could see the sky outside. Evening was setting in.

'The moon will rise soon,' the Baron told him, checking Ulf's chains. 'Wrap more on, Bone. I don't want him breaking free when he transforms.'

Bone wrapped more chains around Ulf and fastened their ends with a padlock. He took the key from the lock and handed it to the Baron.

'Splendid,' Baron Marackai said, slipping the key into the pocket of his fur coat.

Ulf tried to move his arms and legs, but he couldn't.

'There's no point struggling, werewolf,' the Baron said. 'You're not getting out alive.'

Ulf twisted his neck and saw a basket below his head at the end of the bench. It was writhing with rats.

The Baron felt in the basket and pulled out a chewed piece of meat. 'Come and finish your dinner, little rats,' he said. The Baron wiped the meat up and down the rope that secured the guillotine blade.

Ulf saw the rats scurry to the rope. They started chewing it.

'Enjoy your transformation, werewolf. It will be your last,' the Baron said. He rubbed the stump on his right hand where his little finger was missing. 'You've messed up my plans once

too often. But soon I'll be rid of you. Farraway Hall will be mine.'

'Farraway Hall belongs to the RSPCB,' Ulf said. 'Professor Farraway never wanted you to have it.'

The Baron stepped to the door. 'My father was a traitor to the Farraway name,' he spat. 'Come on, Bone. It's time to go hunting.'

Ulf looked up at the blade, then at the rats gnawing the rope. 'Let me out!' he shouted, struggling.

As the Baron and Bone left the room, the Baron glanced over his shoulder. 'Now, now, werewolf. Try not to lose your head.'

He grinned, then slammed the door shut behind him.

★   ★   ★

'Bone, start the machines!' the Baron ordered.

The big man headed off down the corridor to the pedal-carts.

Baron Marackai walked to the archway. He

stood by three levers on the wall, looking into the dungeons.

Blud was revving the engine on his motorbike. The trolls were oofing, reaching through the bars trying to grab Dr Fielding in the blanket of meat. The hunters were waiting with weapons: pistols and rifles, bows and arrows, knives and harpoon guns.

Chuck Armstrong was spinning a pistol on his finger. 'Let's get this party started,' he said.

'Gentlemen, Lady Semolina, if you would join me behind the security door?'

The hunters filed out into the corridor, and the Baron pulled a lever on the wall. Metal bars lowered in the archway, sealing off the dungeons. The hunters peered in through the bars.

'Blud, get ready with the bait!'

Blud revved his engine. He turned the bike to face the end wall of the dungeons, then the Baron pulled a second lever and the end wall started lifting up, revealing the snowy valley outside. It stretched out in front of the dungeons. The snow looked blood-red in the setting sun. Spotlights came on in the valley, lighting up machines and contraptions on either side.

'Behold the Predatron!' the Baron said. 'The most thrilling hunting range known to man.'

Blud sped out on the motorbike, dragging Dr Fielding along the snow wrapped in the blanket of meat.

Baron Marackai pulled a third lever and the doors of the cages sprang open. The trolls bounded out, charging on all fours into the Predatron, following the scent of the meat.

Orson glanced at the Baron. 'You'll pay for this,' he said.

'Hadn't you better save your precious Dr Fielding from those trolls?' the Baron chuckled. 'Run, Mr Orson, run!' The Baron grinned as Orson shook his fist, then strode out into the valley.

'Hunters, proceed to your vehicles!' Baron Marackai said. He turned and marched the hunters down the corridor and through the big wooden door.

Each hunter jumped into a pedal-cart, clutching their weapons.

'Let's hunt these beasts!' the Baron told them. As he stepped into a cart, the Baron felt a tug on his coat. He pulled it into the cart then sat down and pedalled off up the tunnel.

'Yee-ha!' Chuck Armstrong shouted, excitedly.

Lady Semolina blew loudly on a hunting horn.

The Baron rubbed his hands together.

'FIRST STOP: SKITTLE ALLEY!'

CHAPTER SEVENTEEN

Ulf lay beneath the guillotine struggling in the chains. He glanced up at the blade, then across to the rats chewing on the blood-stained rope. Through the open hatch, he could see the sky darkening. Any moment now the full moon would rise.

A trail of sparkles burst through the hatch. It was Tiana!

'Ulf!' she called. 'They've dragged Dr Fielding into the Predatron. They're hunting Orson and the trolls. We've got to do something!'

'I can't move,' Ulf called.

Tiana flew to the guillotine blade. 'Oh my goodness,' she said.

'Quick, stop the rats!' Ulf told her.

Tiana saw the rats gnawing the rope. She flew down and kicked one on the nose. The rat snapped at her tiny foot and she darted out of the way. Tiana grabbed the rat's tail and tugged it, trying to pull the rat from the rope, but the rat flicked its tail sideways, sending her hurtling across the room. Tiana picked herself up from the floor and flew back. Rats were scurrying up and down the rope, gnawing and chewing it. She blasted them with sparkles and they squeaked and scattered. Then they turned and ran back again. 'It's no use, Ulf,' Tiana said, pulling a rat's whiskers. 'I can't stop them!'

The rope was fraying where the rats were chewing it.

Ulf stared at the guillotine blade. 'You have to try,' he said. 'I can't get out.'

He wriggled in the chains, but they were fastened tight. 'I'm locked in,' he said, glancing at the padlock.

Tiana kicked and punched the rats. She blasted and prodded them, but they kept nibbling the rope. 'There are hundreds of them!' she screamed. The rope was creaking, about to snap.

Just then, the door opened. A head poked in with large white eyes, pointy ears and a fat snout.

'Gumball!' Ulf said.

It was the little goblin. He scampered in.

'Oh, that's all we need!' Tiana cried, tugging a rat's ear.

The goblin held out his bony hand. 'Shiny,' he said, smiling. He was holding the key to the padlock!

'Where did you get that?' Ulf asked.

'I took it from the nasty man,' Gumball said, proudly.

The blade was hanging by a single strand.

'Quickly!' Ulf said.

Gumball put the key in the padlock. 'Friend,' he said, turning it.

At that moment, a silvery light shone into the room. Ulf looked up at the open hatch. He could see the moon outside. His eyes flashed silver and he felt the bones in his chest cracking. His skeleton began realigning. Dark hair started growing over his whole body. A thick tail grew from the base of his spine. His nails lengthened into claws. His muscles bulged. Fangs split through his gums. He tore off the chains and sprang forwards just as a rat bit through the last strand of the rope. The guillotine blade slewed down the wooden uprights, thudding into the ground.

Ulf looked out at the moon and howled.

'Gumball, you did it!' Tiana called, flying to the goblin. 'You saved Ulf!'

She planted a kiss on Gumball's fat snout. 'Sorry I was mean to you,' she said.

Gumball blushed.

'The others need saving now,' Ulf growled. He leapt up and scrambled through the open hatch.

'Go, werewolf! Go!' the little goblin called.

Ulf bounded into the Predatron.

CHAPTER EIGHTEEN

In the moonlight, far up ahead, Ulf could see the trolls lumbering through the Predatron. Spotlights shone from the steep slopes on either side of the valley, their beams criss-crossing the snowy ground.

As a wolf, Ulf's senses were sharp. He could smell the trolls' fear. He could hear Baron Marackai's voice: 'Let the fun begin!'

Ulf bounded on all fours, following the meaty trail in the snow where Dr Fielding had been dragged behind the motorbike.

'Be careful, Ulf,' Tiana cried, flying after him.

Ulf scanned the valleysides. He saw Baron Marackai high up, standing by a hatch, holding a megaphone to his mouth. 'Bone, show us the beasts!'

On the side of the valley a spotlight swivelled, sweeping a beam of light on to the trolls. Ulf saw Orson striding after them.

'Release the boulders!' the Baron called. 'Knock them down like skittles!'

Ulf heard a clanking sound and the creaking of levers. He saw a large metal chute pointing down into the valley. It was moving, aiming for the trolls. With a loud rumble, a boulder rolled down the chute. It thundered into the valley and tore across the ground like a huge bowling ball, just missing the trolls.

'Bone! More boulders!' the Baron called.

The metal chute swung sideways, adjusting its aim. A second boulder rolled down and Ulf saw Orson run to protect the trolls. The giant stepped in front of them and smashed the boulder away with his fist. A third boulder came hurtling after. Orson caught it and threw it to the side of the valley. Then he blocked another with his shoulder. Boulder after

boulder came thundering down. Orson tried to block them, but there were too many for him to stop. One of them struck a troll, knocking it to the ground.

'Troll down!' Baron Marackai shouted. 'Guns at the ready!'

Ulf started running for the fallen troll, Tiana whizzing alongside him. He saw five hatches open in the valleyside. The five hunters appeared, each holding a gun. The spotlight shone on the troll.

'Fire!' Marackai commanded.

Shots echoed around the valley and bullets whizzed through the air.

'BANG GOES A TROLL!' the Baron called.

The hunters cheered.

Then the troll sat up, shaking its head.

'It's still alive! You missed!' Baron Marackai called. 'Reload, hunters!'

The hunters took aim at the troll as it was getting to its feet.

'Fire!'

As more shots rang out, Ulf saw Orson

throw himself in front of the troll. The bullets thudded into Orson's chest and he crashed to the ground.

'Bang goes the giant!' the Baron laughed.

'Yee-ha! I got him,' Ulf heard.

'Well done, Mr Armstrong,' the Baron called. 'Hunters, back into your carts. Next stop: the Drowning Pool!'

The hatches slammed shut and the spotlight swivelled, sweeping its beam up the valley.

Ulf raced to Orson. The giant was slumped on the ground. There were bullet holes in his shirt.

'He's dead, Ulf!' Tiana said.

Slowly, Orson sat up. He put his hand inside his shirt and picked out a bullet. He winked at Ulf and smiled. 'Good job I packed my chainmail vest,' he said.

Tiana hugged Orson's ear. 'Thank goodness you're okay.'

Ulf grinned with his fangs. Then he glanced up ahead. He could see the trolls further up the Predatron, sniffing the ground.

'Come on,' he said. 'They're in danger.'

CHAPTER NINETEEN

Ulf raced after the trolls. They were approaching a wide expanse of water that spanned the width of the valley. Ulf could see the meaty trail from Dr Fielding's blanket leading on to a rusty metal bridge.

'Dr Fielding went that way, Tiana,' he said, pointing over the water.

Ulf bounded ahead of the trolls and leapt on to the bridge. He looked down, seeing the full moon reflected below him. Then he felt the bridge wobble and looked back. The trolls were following behind him.

'Ulf, watch out!' Tiana screamed, flying overhead. She pointed across the water.

Standing on the far bank at the end of the bridge was Baron Marackai.

Ulf growled and ran for him.

'What are you doing here, werewolf? You're meant to be dead!' Baron Marackai said. He put the megaphone to his mouth. 'Hunters, we have a new beast in the Predatron. A pesky werewolf!'

The Baron pulled a long lever at the end of the bridge.

Ulf felt the bridge drop away beneath him. He grabbed for the handrail but grasped thin air. He splashed into the cold water below. He kicked his legs, and flicked his tail to swim. He could hear splashing and oofing. The trolls were in the water behind him, thrashing their arms.

'They're drowning!' Tiana cried, flying above them.

'Trolls down!' Ulf heard Baron Marackai call. His voice rang around the valley. 'And the werewolf!'

On the left-hand side of the valley, the hunters stepped out on to a metal balcony.

'Harpoons at the ready!' Baron Marackai called up.

The hunters each pointed a harpoon gun.

'Fire!'

Five metal harpoons whistled through the air and struck the water. A troll squealed.

'Good shot, Herr Pinkel!' the Baron called.

Ulf turned, swimming towards the troll. A harpoon was stuck in its arm. He pulled the harpoon out, then began dragging the troll through the water.

Baron Marackai was looking at Ulf from the shore. 'How dare you, werewolf!' he shouted. 'You're spoiling our fun!'

As Ulf started pushing the troll to the bank, the Baron climbed into a hatch in the ground and disappeared.

The troll slowly pulled itself up and Ulf climbed out after it.

Just then, he heard an almighty splash behind him. Ulf turned and saw Orson wading in the water. The giant was so tall he could stand. He was pushing the other four trolls, two with each arm, towards the shore. 'Stay there, Ulf,' Orson called. 'Help them out.'

Orson lifted a troll from the water and Ulf grabbed its arm.

'Reload and fire again!' he heard. He looked up to the valleyside and saw Baron Marackai appear on the balcony with the hunters.

'Aim for the giant!' the Baron ordered.

'Leave this to me,' Tiana said. She shot over the water and up the valleyside to Lady Semolina. She blew sparkles in the woman's face. Then she flew to Pedro Pedroso and kicked him on the nose. She punched Herman Pinkel in the eye. One by one, the five hunters retreated from the balcony, backing through a door in the side of the valley.

'Come back!' Baron Marackai called. 'It's only a fairy!'

Tiana flew down.

'Thanks, Tiana,' Orson said.

The trolls were lumbering away, sniffing the ground. They were safe – for now.

Baron Marackai clapped his hands. 'Oh, what a bunch of heroes you are,' he called. 'Well, let's see how you deal with the Forest of Fear.'

He left the balcony, disappearing into the valleyside.

Orson pulled himself out of the Drowning Pool and sat on the bank. He took off his boots and tipped them up. Icy water poured out. 'Bit nippy for a swim,' he said.

Ulf looked up the Predatron. The trolls were moving towards a silvery forest. 'Let's go!' he said, bounding after them.

Tiana raced alongside him. 'Hurry up, Orson,' she called.

The giant was pulling his boots on, hobbling behind. 'I'm coming as fast as I can.'

CHAPTER TWENTY

The Forest of Fear was made of metal. Ulf padded between tall trees of twisted iron, their spiked branches blocking out the moonlight. He ducked under rusting leaves and crept past bushes of barbed wire, peering into the shadows. He could hear the trolls snuffling up ahead, following the scent of the meat.

'Be careful,' Orson whispered, pushing through the metal branches.

'It's creepy in here,' Tiana said. 'I don't like it.'

Ulf moved stealthily, his paws scrunching in the snow. Suddenly, he heard a twanging sound and an arrow whizzed through the branches. 'Hunters,' he said, crouching low.

'Where are they?' Tiana asked, darting behind a rusty leaf. 'I can't see them.'

Another arrow whistled through the trees. The trolls roared and Ulf heard them clattering through the metal undergrowth, scattering in all directions.

Orson strode off. 'Keep with them,' he said, pushing through the forest, snapping the iron branches with his bare hands.

To his left, Ulf heard a loud squeal and a crash of metal. He rushed towards the sound and saw a big net swinging from a tree. A troll was trapped in it.

A hatch sprang open by a bush and Biggy popped up, aiming a longbow and arrow. He fired at the troll and the beast roared.

Ulf leapt for the hunter.

'Holy hotdogs!' Biggy cried, seeing Ulf coming for him.

Biggy ducked back underground, slamming the metal hatch behind him. Ulf landed with a thud on top of the hatch and tried to prise it open. It was stuck. He could hear a bolt

being drawn underground then the squeaking pedals of a cart trundling away beneath the forest floor.

'Up here, Ulf!' Tiana called. She was circling the troll in the net.

Ulf leapt up and slashed the net with his claws, cutting the troll free. It landed with a thud in the snow then stood up, staring at Ulf with wide eyes. It was a young male and looked frightened.

'Do not fear me,' Ulf growled. He gently bit the arrow in the troll's leg and pulled it out with his teeth. The troll grunted then lumbered away through the forest, sniffing the snow.

Ulf heard the Baron's voice again, calling: 'Get the werewolf!'

A hatch opened in the metal trunk of a tree. Pedro Pedroso popped out, aiming a crossbow. He fired at Ulf. Ulf dodged and an arrow shot past him, just clipping his bushy tail. The hatch in the tree slammed shut and Ulf heard the hunter climbing down a metal ladder underground. Ulf bounded away on all fours.

'Watch out!' Tiana called, flying after him.

The sharp point of another arrow flashed in the moonlight. Ulf ducked and it ricocheted off a metal branch. Then a knife flew past, spinning through the air. It landed in a barbed-wire bush. Ulf kept low as he raced through the trees, until finally he saw moonlight ahead.

He found Orson at the edge of the forest, trying to calm a troll. The giant was pulling netting from its tusks.

'Easy there, girl. We'll get you out of here,' the giant said. The troll grunted as Orson let it go. It lumbered out of the forest, following Dr Fielding's scent.

'Orson, are they all okay?' Tiana asked.

'They all made it,' the giant said.

Below ground, Ulf could hear pedal-carts squeaking. The hunters were moving up the Predatron. 'It's not over yet,' he warned.

CHAPTER TWENTY-ONE

Ulf sprinted ahead of Orson and Tiana, trying to catch up with the trolls.

The valley narrowed to a thin passageway between sheer metal walls over thirty metres high. It was illuminated by a string of electric light bulbs. The trolls were funnelling into it, sniffing in a line. Ulf ran in after them.

'Bone, start the Crusher!' he heard. Baron Marackai was standing at the very top of the right-hand wall, peering down.

From behind the metal walls came the rumbling sounds of engines. Clumps of snow began falling into the valley as the walls started moving inwards. Up ahead, the trolls began roaring. The passageway was narrowing. The trolls started oofing, beating their fists against the walls. The Crusher was trapping them.

'Hunters, load your weapons!' Baron Marackai called.

Ulf looked up and saw five guns pointing down.

'Take aim! F—'

Suddenly, there was a loud clang and the wrenching sound of straining metal pistons.

'Blud! Bone! What's happening?' Baron Marackai called.

Something was wrong with the Crusher.

Ulf looked back. Orson was at the entrance, pulling the metal walls apart with his mighty hands. Tiana was hovering above him. 'Heave, Orson! Heave!' she cried.

Ulf could hear the engines grinding. There was a sputtering sound then a loud bang as the Crusher broke and the lights went out. The walls started edging apart.

'Quick, fire at will!' the Baron called.

The hunters' guns blasted, but as the trolls

ran out, the bullets missed, sparking on the metal walls.

Orson came striding towards Ulf. 'Nothing's stronger than a giant,' he said.

Ulf looked up. He saw Baron Marackai silhouetted against the full moon. The Baron was shaking his fist. 'You and your miserable friends, werewolf! I'll get you!' he spat. 'It's time for war!'

The Baron fired an orange flare into the sky. It hung in the air, lighting the valley ahead. Ulf hurried out of the Crusher and in the orange light he could see the trolls sniffing through a wide section of the Predatron, following the meaty trail in the snow.

The Baron appeared on a balcony at the side of the valley and raised his megaphone. 'Let battle commence!'

Five hatches opened in the valleyside and the hunters threw hand grenades down. The grenades blasted huge craters in the snow.

The trolls started stampeding. A metal disc sprang up from the ground, tossing a troll into the air. Ulf heard the whizz of bullets, then a thud as the troll landed. It stood up, its legs wobbling.

'Missed!' Baron Marackai called. 'Can't you hit a moving target? Bone, fix the trolls to the spot! Start the Sticky Stucky!'

A large tube poked out from the hillside. It blasted a volley of black balls. They burst as they landed, splattering pools of glue on the ground. A troll ran into the glue. Its feet stuck and it roared with rage as it tried to move.

'That's it,' the Baron called. 'Now roll the logs, Blud!'

Tree trunks began tumbling down the valleyside. They knocked a troll to the ground.

'Now turn on the gas!' Baron Marackai called.

Ulf heard a hissing sound and columns of yellow gas shot up from pipes in the ground. The gas drifted across the valley, stinging Ulf's eyes. Ahead he could make out a troll crawling from the gas, tears streaming down its face.

'Boo hoo hooo,' Baron Marackai called. 'Start the Demolition Ball!'

There was a loud cranking sound. In the centre of the valley Ulf saw the tall pole with the huge metal ball attached by a chain. The pole began turning. The metal ball began swinging on its chain. It swung in circles, skimming the snow, faster and faster. The metal ball struck a troll and sent it flying.

'Start the Claw!' Baron Marackai called.

At the side of the valley Ulf saw the crane with the mechanical claw. Its long metal arm was moving, lowering the claw to the ground. The claw closed around the troll's leg, then lifted it up and dangled it above the valley.

A second orange flare went off in the sky. The trolls were roaring: stuck in glue, choking on gas, springing through the air and dazed from the Demolition Ball and rolling logs.

'Hunters, kill at will!' the Baron called.

'Ulf, we've got to save them!' Tiana cried.

Ulf snarled. 'It's time to hunt the hunters!'

CHAPTER TWENTY-TWO

Ulf scanned the valley, locating the hunters. He saw Pedro Pedroso at a hatch high up in the side of the valley. Ulf bounded across the snow on all fours. He leapt on to a metal disc and a spring pinged him towards the valleyside. He struck the metal wall, gripping with his claws. Above him, he saw Pedro Pedroso loading a rifle. Ulf climbed up to the hatch and lunged for the gun, biting it in half with his teeth.

The hunter screamed. 'Ay Carumba!'

Ulf reached into the hatch and pulled Pedro Pedroso out by his ponytail. Pedro Pedroso tumbled head over heels down the valleyside and into the snow. He landed in a pool of glue. He tried to get up but he was stuck. 'Ayuda! Sticky stucky!' he shouted.

Tiana flew over to the hunter and blasted him with her sparkles. 'Go, Ulf!' she called.

Ulf pulled himself through the hatch. Now he was back inside the workings of the Predatron. He dropped on to the metal tracks and followed them along the tunnel. Ahead, he could see a pedal-cart parked and Herman Pinkel leaning out through a hatch. Ulf crept up quietly behind the hunter and snarled.

Herman Pinkel turned. 'Achtung Volf!' the hunter cried, dropping his rifle. He stepped back, his legs trembling, and fell on to a stack of tree trunks at the side of the tunnel.

'Fun's over,' Ulf growled. He pulled a lever and the wall of the tunnel swung open. The tree trunks thundered out, taking Herman Pinkel with them.

'Ouch! Oo! Argh!' the hunter cried, as he tumbled down into the valley.

Ulf licked his fangs.

'Over here, Ulf,' Tiana called, hovering above a hatch that was opening in the snowy ground. Chuck Armstrong popped up from the hatch, spinning two pistols on his fingers. He pointed them at a troll as it lumbered through the yellow gas.

Ulf turned and bounded along the track inside the Predatron. He saw a sign marked **GAS ATTACK** and raced steeply downwards under the valley. In a tunnel ahead of him, he saw Chuck Armstrong's legs. The hunter was standing at the top of a ladder.

He heard the hunter shooting. Ulf dived to a gas pipe at the base of the ladder and bit it in two. A jet of yellow gas shot up, blasting Chuck Armstrong out through the hatch. Ulf scrambled up the ladder and saw the hunter crawling in the snow surrounded by gas.

He was crying like a baby. 'I want my mummy.'

Ulf saw the troll lumbering away. Chuck Armstrong had missed.

He looked for Tiana and saw a flash of

flames burst in the distance. Up the valley Biggy was holding a flame-thrower, running towards a troll. It had been hit by the Demolition Ball and was stumbling, dazed.

Suddenly, Biggy stopped. A sparkle was darting around his head. Ulf smiled. Tiana was attacking the hunter. Flames shot high into the air as the big man staggered in the snow, trying to blast the fairy with his flame-thrower. Tiana swooped and dodged.

'Go, Tiana!' Ulf called.

The Demolition Ball was circling. Orson strode over and grabbed hold of it. He swung the ball towards Biggy.

Tiana zoomed away and the Demolition Ball smashed into the big man.

'Aaghhhhhhhh!' Biggy called, hurtling across the valley.

Ulf heard Baron Marackai's voice from the valleyside: 'You wretched, horrible, meddling beasts!'

The Baron was spitting with fury. 'Shoot them all, Lady Semolina!'

Lady Semolina was on a balcony swivelling a machine gun into position.

'No you don't,' Ulf growled. He raced across the valley towards the Claw. He leapt into the control cabin, and pulled a lever. The crane arm extended. He pulled another and the arm swung above the balcony. He pulled a third and the metal claw opened.

As Lady Semolina started firing, Ulf lowered the metal claw on to her, closing it around her waist. He lifted her off the bridge and swung her over the valley.

'Help me!' she cried, her legs jiggling in the air.

Ulf sprang from the crane and snarled.

'Nice work, Ulf,' Orson called. The giant came striding to Ulf's side. Tiana came flying after.

'That showed those hunters,' the fairy said.

'You haven't won yet!' the Baron shouted. He was pointing to the far end of the valley. 'Aren't you forgetting dear Dr Fielding?'

The five trolls were up ahead, following

the meaty trail through the snow. They were heading towards a big metal archway with coloured lights flashing around its edge. The lights spelt out the words **FEEDING TROUGH**.

'IT'S TIME FOR THE TROLLS' SUPPER!' the Baron called.

CHAPTER TWENTY-THREE

'You save Dr Fielding,' Orson said to Ulf. 'Leave the trolls to me.'

Ulf bounded past the trolls and headed through the metal archway into a tall tunnel. He glanced back. Orson was blocking the entrance, stopping the trolls coming in. The giant's chainmail vest rattled as the trolls butted and charged him. 'Now there's no need for that,' Orson said.

Tiana flew among the trolls, shining her light in their eyes. 'You're not allowed in there.'

'Good thinking, Tiana,' Orson said. 'Keep them back.'

Ulf sprinted through the tunnel and out the

169

other side into a round snowy expanse with sheer metal walls. He saw balconies, and a ring of floodlights lighting up the snow. In the centre of the valley, a large metal feeding trough lay on the ground. Beyond it were the entrances to dark tunnels. He looked up. He was facing Honeycomb Mountain. Its silhouette loomed over the end of the valley a hundred metres high.

Ulf saw something move in the feeding trough. Lying there, wrapped in the blanket of meat, was Dr Fielding. She was gagged and struggling, tied up in ropes and chains. He ran towards her.

'Going somewhere, werewolf?' he heard.

Ulf looked up. Baron Marackai was standing on a balcony, holding his megaphone to his mouth.

Ulf snarled.

'You're going the wrong way,' the Baron called. 'It's Mr Orson who's going to die first. Blud! Bone! Bury the giant!'

Ulf glanced back at the archway. Shards of

metal flew across the valley as it exploded in a flash of bright flames. A shockwave punched Ulf's chest, knocking him to the ground. He watched in horror as a cloud of smoke rose into the air, revealing a massive mound of snow and twisted iron. The archway had collapsed. Orson was buried beneath it.

'Orson!' Ulf cried, scrambling to his feet. He raced back and began digging frantically, pulling out twisted iron girders and throwing them aside.

Tiana flew up from behind the mound. 'Orson!' she was calling.

Ulf heaved aside a girder and saw the tip of Orson's finger poking out from underneath. He cleared the metal and snow from around the giant's hand. 'Orson, get up!' he called.

The hand lay heavy and still.

Tiana perched on Orson's fingertip. 'No!' she cried. 'Poor Orson.' A tear rolled down her cheek.

Ulf looked up. He could hear the trolls clambering up the far side of the mound, sniffing and grunting. They were coming for their dinner.

'Save Dr Fielding…!' Tiana cried.

There was nothing Ulf could do for Orson now. He turned back and ran towards the Feeding Trough.

From the balcony, the Baron called through his megaphone: 'Blud! Bone! Stop the werewolf!'

Below the Baron, a metal door opened and Blud and Bone stepped out on to the snow. The big man was holding an iron bar, and the small man was cowering behind him.

'You get him, Bone,' Blud said.

Ulf snarled as the big man came running towards him.

Bone swung the iron bar.

Ulf dodged, and the bar whipped past his ear, just clipping his fur.

Blud kept hidden behind Bone. 'That's it, sock it to him,' the small man said.

Bone swung the iron bar again.

Ulf dived to the side, landing in the snow.

The big man stood over him, clutching the iron bar in both hands.

'Now you've got him. Knock him out,' Blud said, peeking from between Bone's legs.

As the iron bar came thumping down into the snow, Ulf rolled. He leapt up, grabbed the bar in his jaws and bit it in two.

'Bloomin' heck,' Bone said, stepping back.

Ulf snarled at the big man, showing his fangs.

'Now what do I do, Blud?' Bone asked.

'Run!' Blud yelled.

Both men started running back to the door in the valleyside.

'Come back, you pathetic cowards!' Baron Marackai cried.

Blud and Bone raced through the door, slamming it shut behind them.

'I'll deal with you myself, werewolf!' the Baron called.

Ulf glanced across and saw the Baron jumping off the balcony into the snow. Then he heard trolls grunting. He glanced back at the fallen archway. The trolls had climbed over the mound and were heading for the Feeding Trough. Ulf leapt to Dr Fielding. He bit through the chains and ropes around her, then ripped off the blanket of meat.

She pulled off her gag. 'Thank you, Ulf!' she gasped, climbing out of the Feeding Trough.

'No you don't, werewolf!' Ulf heard.

On the far side of the trough, a hatch opened in the ground. Baron Marackai stepped out, pointing a pistol at Ulf. 'Now *you* can die!' he said.

As the Baron pulled the trigger, Ulf dived for cover into the Feeding Trough. The bullet ricocheted off the metal.

'Leave him alone!' Dr Fielding cried.

'Oh, okay, if you insist,' the Baron said. 'I shall leave him to the trolls instead.' The Baron started laughing. 'HA HA HAAA HAA HAAAAAAA HAAAAAAAAAAAAAAA!'

Ulf peered out of the trough.

All five trolls were thundering towards him, slobbering. Ulf was lying with the meaty steaks!

Ulf leapt up and threw the blanket of meat over Baron Marackai. It landed on the Baron's head, covering him completely. Dr Fielding stepped forwards holding a chain, and looped it over the Baron's shoulders. She pulled it tight. The Baron struggled, hopping up and down, trying to wriggle out of the blanket of meat. 'Nooooooo!' he cried.

He started running away as the hungry trolls thundered past the Feeding Trough, chasing him.

Ulf and Dr Fielding watched as the Baron ran towards Honeycomb Mountain, the blanket of meat over his head. He smacked into the base of the mountain and fell backwards. Then he got up, his legs wobbling. He was feeling his way along the wall.

The trolls were charging on all fours towards him, gouging the air with their tusks.

The Baron reached a tunnel and ran inside. The trolls ran in after him. Ulf could hear their hungry grunts echoing as the Baron screamed: 'I'll be baaaaaack!'

Ulf watched, panting.

'Where's Orson?' Dr Fielding asked.

Ulf looked back at the mound of metal and snow where the archway had fallen. He could see Tiana's light glowing above Orson's finger. 'I couldn't save him,' Ulf replied.

As he stared at the mound, Ulf heard a rumble. The snow and metal started moving.

Orson was rising from beneath it.

Tiana flew up, sparkling. 'Orson's alive!' she called.

The giant rubbed his head and looked around. 'Has anyone seen those trolls?' he asked.

Ulf smiled, his fangs glinting. He looked up at the moon and howled.

CHAPTER TWENTY-FOUR

The next day, Ulf woke late with the sun on his face. He opened his eyes. He was back in his den at Farraway Hall. Folded outside his door were a pair of jeans and a T-shirt. He pulled them on and stepped out into the sunshine.

Tiana came flying from the paddock. 'Good afternoon, Ulf,' she said. 'You were brilliant last night!'

Ulf rubbed his eyes. 'Was I?' he asked.

'Don't you remember? You stopped the troll hunt. You saved Dr Fielding.'

Ulf licked his teeth. His fangs had receded back into his gums. The memory of his transformation was a blur.

'How did we get home?' he asked.

'Orson straightened the helicopter blades and we flew back this morning. After waiting for you, of course. You went wild last night, chasing snow hares. Dr Fielding let you loose in the mountains.'

Ulf smiled.

'Come on. Dr Fielding asked me to come and get you,' Tiana said.

The fairy flew off and Ulf followed her up the side of the paddock into the yard.

'Afternoon, Ulf,' he heard.

Orson came out of the feedstore. The giant had a crutch under his arm made from a tree trunk, and a bandage wrapped around his head.

'Are you okay, Orson?' Ulf asked.

'Nothing that a barrel of apples and a bucket of tea won't mend. You were brave last night, Ulf. You showed those hunters.'

'They'll all be behind bars by now,' Dr Fielding said, stepping out from the side-door of Farraway Hall. 'The department for

National and International Criminal Emergencies were very interested to hear what they'd been up to.'

'NICE?' Ulf said.

'I called NICE from Loadem Lodge. They've arrested the hunters and are dismantling the Predatron.'

Dr Fielding was carrying the bat-cage with Gumball's messenger bat inside. She smiled at Ulf. 'Thank you for saving me last night,' she said. She put the bat-cage down and gave Ulf a big hug.

'That's okay, Dr Fielding,' Ulf said, wriggling away.

He looked at the bat. It was nibbling a grasshopper, feeding up for its journey home. 'I couldn't have done it without Gumball. Gumball rescued me.'

'It seems Professor Farraway knew what he was doing, making Gumball a spotter,' Dr Fielding said. She glanced at Tiana and winked.

'I still think he smells.' Tiana giggled.

Dr Fielding knelt down and opened the door of the bat-cage. 'Would you like to release the messenger bat, Ulf?' she asked.

Ulf reached in and picked up Gumball's bat.

'One moment, Ulf,' Dr Fielding said. From the pocket of her white coat she took out a scrap of paper. On it, she'd written, *Thank You*.

Dr Fielding slipped the message into the ring on the bat's leg then Ulf released it into the air. He watched as it circled high above the yard then flew off over Farraway Hall.

'Bye bye, batty!' Ulf heard. Druce the gargoyle was bounding along the rooftop, waving.

Ulf watched the bat fly away until it was a tiny dot in the distance. 'What about the trolls?' he asked Dr Fielding.

'Trolls are tough beasts. They'll be fine,' she told him. 'Those young ones will be safely back with their families by now.'

Ulf wondered if they'd eaten the Baron.

'There's something I don't quite understand,' he said. 'How did Marackai know about the Predatron?'

Dr Fielding glanced at Orson. Orson nodded. 'I think there's something you should see, Ulf,' she said.

Ulf followed Dr Fielding into her office.

'You'd better sit down, Ulf. I'm afraid this is quite shocking.' On Dr Fielding's desk was a leatherbound photograph album. 'We found this at Loadem Lodge.'

Ulf sat in the chair at Dr Fielding's desk. He opened the album and started turning the pages. Ulf saw old black-and-white photographs. 'This is horrible,' he said.

In each photograph, a hunter was holding up the head of a dead beast mounted on a plaque like a trophy. There were troll heads... griffin heads... giranha heads... jackalope heads... and in one of the pictures a hunter was holding the head of a werewolf.

Ulf felt sick. 'How can humans be so cruel?' he asked.

'Those hunters aren't just any humans, Ulf. They're all Farraways,' Dr Fielding said. 'They're the Professor's ancestors.'

'Professor Farraway?' Ulf asked.

'The Professor was born into a long line of hunters, Ulf.'

'I don't understand,' Ulf said. 'The Professor was a good man.'

Dr Fielding turned the pages in the album to a photograph of a man standing beside a single metal tree. 'This man is the Professor's great-great-grandfather,' she said. 'It seems he built the Predatron.'

The man's face looked twisted and mean.

'Professor Farraway wasn't like the rest of his family, Ulf. He stopped the Predatron when he inherited the Farraway estate. He set up the RSPCB to protect beasts and to make amends for what his ancestors had done.'

Ulf felt shocked. 'You mean all the Farraways were bad?'

Then he remembered being chained to the guillotine. Marackai had called the Professor a traitor to the Farraway name.

'It wasn't Marackai who was the disgrace to the Farraway family, Ulf. It was the Professor.'

Dr Fielding closed the photograph album. 'It's over now, though,' she said. 'Marackai's gone, thanks to you.'

Dr Fielding whistled and the Helping Hand scuttled in. 'File this under Historical Hunting, will you please?'

The Helping Hand took the photograph album and carried it to a cupboard at the back of the room.

Dr Fielding opened her office door and Ulf followed her into the corridor. 'You should do something fun today, Ulf. You've had a tough night.'

'I'm okay,' Ulf said.

She ruffled his hair. 'Why don't you come to the hatching bay with me? We've got some jellystoats that are due to be born any moment.'

'I will in a bit,' Ulf told her. 'There's something I need to do first.'

Dr Fielding headed down the corridor. 'Okay, I'll see you later.'

Ulf ran up the back stairs. He raced through the Room of Curiosities and opened the library door. It was dark inside. 'Professor, are you in here?' he asked.

On a table by the end wall, a candle flickered on, lighting up a portrait of Professor Farraway. 'I know about your family,' Ulf said.

He stared at the painting, looking at the Professor's kind eyes. 'I've come to tell you that the Predatron's being dismantled,' he said. 'Marackai's gone.'

But as Ulf spoke, he felt an icy chill pass through him. The candle rose into the air.

'It's okay, Professor. It's over.'

The candle was drifting to the window. Ulf saw the corner of the curtain peeling back, revealing daylight and the beast park outside.

'We're safe, Professor,' he said. Then the hairs on Ulf's neck stood on end as an invisible finger began writing on the dusty glass: *BE ON YOUR GUARD. NO BEAST IS SAFE FROM HIM*

THE END ... FOR NOW

Visit www.beastlybusiness.com
for lots of exciting **extras**
- meet the **authors**, join the
RSPCB and discover the **secrets**
of the **beasts**...!

SIMON AND SCHUSTER
A CBS Company

**Turn the page for the first
two exciting chapters from
*The Jungle Vampire***

CHAPTER ONE

Late one night, on the outskirts of a grimy town, a man in a long fur coat hurried through the rain. He held a black umbrella, hiding his face in shadow as he passed beneath the street lamps and turned down a quiet backstreet. He strode to the door of a warehouse, looked left then right, then knocked three times.

From inside came a voice: 'Who goes there?'

'It's me, you fool,' the man hissed. 'Open up.'

There came a scraping sound of a bolt being slid across. The door squeaked open and in the entrance to the warehouse stood a small man in a ragged suit. 'Sorry, Baron Marackai. You said not to let anyone in.'

'I meant strangers, Blud, you imbecile!'

Baron Marackai barged inside and whacked the small man with his umbrella. 'Well? Is it ready?' he asked.

'Not yet, Sir,' Blud replied.

The Baron looked to the end of the warehouse where a rickety flying machine was being assembled. It had two black wings and an open cockpit with a machine gun mounted to its front. Crawling over it were a dozen Helping Hands, small hand-shaped beasts, clutching spanners, tightening nuts and bolts.

'*Why* isn't it finished?' Baron Marackai yelled. 'It's supposed to be a *quick-assembly* flying machine!'

A big, bearded man was standing at the end of the warehouse holding a long whip. 'The little blighters won't do as they're told, Sir,' he said.

'Then whip them harder, Bone, you wimp!' The Baron marched over and snatched the big man's whip. He cracked it against the knuckles of a Helping Hand. 'Work faster!' he ordered it.

'I don't think they like being whipped, Sir,' Bone said.

'Good,' Baron Marackai replied. He cracked the whip again, even harder. The Helping Hand flinched, then it hurriedly began tightening a row of screws along the wing of the flying machine. Other Helping Hands scuttled to assist it. Two bolted a propeller to the front of the flying machine and more attached wheels to its base.

'That's more like it,' the Baron said. He paced around the machine, inspecting it closely. 'The perfect weapon,' he muttered.

The small man, Blud, scuttled over and tugged on the Baron's wet fur coat. 'Excuse me, Sir, but why do we need a flying machine?'

The Baron swivelled the gun on its front. 'Because we're going hunting.'

'Hunting for what, Sir?' Blud asked.

The Baron stroked the barrel of the gun. 'We're going hunting for a beast,' he said. 'A beast more terrifying than any you could possibly imagine.' He leant down to Blud, his twisted face grinning. 'And when we find it, we're going to kill it.'

Blud smiled nervously. 'But what about you-know-who, Sir?' he asked.

'Those fools? Pa!' the Baron spat. 'They'll never catch us.' He raised his right hand. There was a small fleshy stump where his little finger was missing. 'Now repeat after me: death to the RSPCB!'

Blud and Bone raised their right hands and turned down their little fingers. 'Death to the RSPCC,' they mumbled.

'The RSPC*B*, you nincompoops!'

The Baron snatched a Helping Hand from the flying machine and slapped it across Blud's face. Then he poked Bone in the eye with its finger. 'Well, don't just stand there! Get ready!' he ordered. 'WE FLY TONIGHT!'

CHAPTER TWO

Two days later, at the Royal Society for the Prevention of Cruelty to Beasts, Ulf was in the big beast barn tending to a pegasaur. The winged horse had been brought into the rescue centre after its nest had become waterlogged in recent rains. It was suffering from a case of hoof-rot. Ulf had scrubbed its hooves with a wire brush and was filing them carefully with a metal rasp.

The RSPCB cared for all kinds of beasts, from sick sea monsters to trolls with toothache, from frostbitten dragons to fairies with broken wings. Ulf enjoyed helping to mend them.

He sprayed the pegasaur's hooves with antifungal spray, then checked its hairy white wings for lice and ticks. 'You'll be as good as new soon,' he said to it. He gave it some hay to eat, then stepped out into the yard, closing the wooden doors behind him.

'Fur Face want some?' he heard. Ulf glanced up at Farraway Hall, a large country mansion – the headquarters of the RSPCB. On the rooftop, a gargoyle was picking earwax from its ear. 'Fur Face want some?' the gargoyle said again. It leered down and flicked the earwax at Ulf.

Ulf dodged. 'Missed me, Druce,' he said, laughing. Quickly, Ulf ran to the yard tap to wash his hands. He could hear the gargoyle gurgling. It was eating its breakfast, licking its ear with its yellow tongue. He could hear beasts in the beast park, roaring and squawking. The rains had stopped and they were enjoying the sunshine. Ulf smiled. It was a bright, cheery day.

To look at Ulf, washing his hands and drying them on his T-shirt, it would be easy to mistake him for a human boy. But if you looked closely, you'd notice the hair on his palms. For Ulf was a beast himself. Every month, on the night of the full moon, he'd transform from boy to wolf. Ulf was a werewolf.

He glanced across the yard to the feedstore, a tall wooden building with double doors. The doors were open, and inside he could see Orson the giant loading a huge rucksack with tins. Ulf went to see him. 'What are you doing, Orson?' he asked, peering in the doorway.

The giant looked over. 'Just getting something ready for Dr Fielding,' he replied.

Ulf glanced back towards Farraway Hall. Through a window on the ground floor, he could see Dr Fielding in her office. 'She's been in there all morning,' Ulf said. 'And last night. I saw her light on. What's she up to?'

'I'm afraid I'm not to say, Ulf,' the giant told him.

'Not to say *what*?'

Ulf saw the giant open the meats fridge and take out six packs of sausages.

'Sorry, Ulf, I can't chat now. There's lots to do before we go.'

'Go?' Ulf asked. 'Go where?'

The giant chuckled. 'Like I said, I'm not to tell. Top secret it is. Dr Fielding's orders.' He carried the rucksack to the back of the feedstore and began looking along the shelves, whistling to himself.

Ulf glanced back to Dr Fielding's office. The window was open. He crept across the yard, keeping low, and peered over the window ledge. A bright sparkle was hovering above Dr Fielding's desk. It was Tiana the fairy, Ulf's best friend. He listened, hearing Dr Fielding talking to her.

'You'll love it there, Tiana,' Dr Fielding said. 'There'll be all kinds of flowers with rare pollens to collect, so be sure to bring your satchel.'

'I'll fetch it right away,' Tiana replied. In a burst of sparkles the little fairy flew out through the window, zooming over Ulf's head.

'Psst,' he said to her.

Tiana stopped in mid-air. 'Ulf, are you snooping?' she whispered. The fairy swooped down and perched on his shoulder. She was dressed in camouflage, wearing a new dress made from blades of grass and creeper twine.

'You're all going somewhere, aren't you?' Ulf asked.

Tiana giggled. 'Whatever gave you that idea?'

Ulf eyed the fairy suspiciously, then peered back over the window ledge and saw Dr Fielding stand up and take an empty mug from her desk. She walked to the door and left her office. Quickly, he climbed in through the window to see what she'd been up to.

'Ulf, you shouldn't go in there,' Tiana called.

Ulf crept to Dr Fielding's desk. It was strewn with books, maps and RSPCB papers. A magazine was laid open at a page with a photograph of butterflies ringed in red pen. Ulf picked the magazine up. Beneath the photograph he read a caption:

Speckled Bluetails at Drake's Ridge, emailed from the Maripossa Mountains by butterfly photographer Hurricane Stoat

Ulf looked back at Tiana who was hovering

at the windowsill. 'Why's she reading about butterflies?' he asked.

Tiana twiddled a blade of grass on her dress. 'Maybe she likes them,' she said cagily.

Ulf heard footsteps coming back down the corridor. Hurriedly, he crawled under the desk to hide. He peeked out, seeing Dr Fielding's boots as she came back in. She walked over, and he heard her place her mug on the desk.

'Tiana, have you seen my copy of *Wildlife Weekly*?' Dr Fielding asked.

Ulf heard Tiana giggling on the windowsill. He had the magazine in his hand. A moment later, Dr Fielding's face appeared under the desk and he smiled, embarrassed.

'Cosy down there, are you, Ulf?' she asked.

'The game's up, werewolf,' Tiana said, laughing.

Ulf crawled out and handed Dr Fielding the magazine. 'I was only er... um...'

Dr Fielding frowned at him. 'Snooping, it's called, Ulf.'

'Sorry, Dr Fielding.'

Dr Fielding took a sip from her mug of coffee and smiled. 'Well, seeing as you're here, there's something I'd like to show you.' She picked up a dusty folder from her desk and handed it to him. 'This is one of Professor Farraway's old expedition files.'

Ulf held the folder excitedly. Professor Farraway had been the world's first cryptozoologist and the founder of the RSPCB. On the front of the folder Ulf saw EXPEDITION MANCHAY written in the Professor's handwriting. 'What's Manchay?' he asked.

'Manchay is a wild beast habitat, Ulf,' Dr Fielding told him. 'It's a remote jungle in South America.'

Ulf opened the folder. Inside were photographs of jungle beasts: winged beasts, armoured beasts, aquatic beasts and more.

'It's also one of the only places on earth where beasts and humans have lived together,' Dr Fielding added.

'Humans? Living with beasts?' Ulf said.

'Thousands of years ago, Manchay was home to a human tribe,' Dr Fielding explained. She picked out a photograph of gravestones overgrown with jungle vines and creepers. 'This is their burial ground, Ulf.'

In the photograph, among the graves, Ulf could see ghostly shadows with hollow eyes.

'Those are called encantos,' Dr Fielding said. 'They're the spirits of the ancient tribe. Professor Farraway photographed them on his expedition.'

Ulf looked closely at the photograph, imagining the spirits as a human tribe thousands of years ago living in the jungle.

'The Professor is the only person to have set foot in Manchay for centuries. He'd heard stories of spine-tingling screeches coming from the jungle at night. He had a theory that they were the cries of a very rare beast.'

'What beast?' Ulf asked.

'A jungle vampire,' Dr Fielding said.

'A *vampire*?'

Ulf had never seen a vampire before. He looked through the photographs searching for a picture of it. 'I can't see it here,' he said.

'That's because the Professor returned without finding it. I'd always assumed that maybe it didn't exist – until now.' Dr Fielding opened her copy of *Wildlife Weekly* and turned to the page showing the photograph of the butterflies ringed in red pen. 'Have a look at this, Ulf. This picture was taken by a photographer named Hurricane Stoat on a mountain range overlooking Manchay.'

'Butterflies?' Ulf asked.

'Look at the rock they're settled on.'

Ulf looked carefully. On the rock, between the butterflies, he could just make out faint carved lines.

'That's a tribal carving, Ulf.'

The lines formed an image of a winged beast with fangs.

'It's a vampire,' Dr Fielding said. 'The tribe must have known of the beast. I think it could still be out there.'

Ulf looked up from the photograph. 'After all this time?'

'Vampires can live indefinitely if there's blood for them to drink,' Dr Fielding told him. 'What do you say we go and look for it?'

'We?' Ulf asked.

'I've been observing you recently, Ulf, and I think you're ready to begin your training.'

'What training?'

'To become an official RSPCB agent. If that's what you'd like.'

'Yes, please!' Ulf said excitedly.

'Manchay will be the perfect place for you to learn about jungle beasts.'

Ulf could hardly believe what he was hearing. Dr Fielding never normally invited him on expeditions to the wild. He'd been just once, to the Jotunheim mountains of Norway, and only then because he'd stowed away.

'The search for the vampire should be quite an adventure, Ulf. Tiana will be coming.'

Ulf looked across at the little fairy perched on the windowsill.

'Surprise,' she giggled.

'I knew something was going on,' Ulf said.

'Orson's coming too,' Dr Fielding told him. Outside in the yard, Ulf could see Orson striding to the kit room. The giant was carrying his rucksack on his back. 'Why don't you go and help get the kit ready, Ulf.' Dr Fielding glanced at her wristwatch. 'We're due to leave in twenty minutes.'